ROCKABYE MURDER

A MATERNAL INSTINCTS MYSTERY

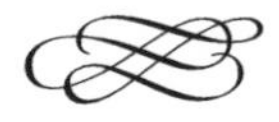

DIANA ORGAIN

OTHER TITLES BY DIANA ORGAIN

Maternal Instincts Mystery Series

Bundle of Trouble - FREE The only thing tougher than solving a murder… giving birth!

Motherhood is Murder Kate joins a new mom group where mischief and murder run rampant.

Formula for Murder A hit and run crash catapults Kate into a mystery at the French Consulate.

Nursing a Grudge Kate's budding PI business is threatened when a new PI poaches her client.

Pampered to Death Spa day has never been so deadly!

Killer Cravings Can Kate juggle being a PI, pregnant and those cravings all at the same time?

A Deathly Rattle Who shot rival PI, Vicente Domingo?

Rockabye Murder Dancing can be murder—literally.

Prams & Poison Are there too many skeletons in the Victorian closet Paula's is renovating?

Love or Money Mystery Series

A First Date with Death Reality TV meets murder!

A Second Chance at Murder Georgia's new boyfriend disappears in the Pyrenees Mountains.

Third Time's a Crime If only love were as simple as murder…

ROUNDUP CREW MYSTERY SERIES

Yappy Hour Things take a *ruff* turn at the Wine & Bark when Maggie Patterson takes charge

Trigger Yappy Salmonella poisoning strikes at the Wine & Bark.

IWITCH MYSTERY SERIES

A Witch Called Wanda Can a witch solve a murder mystery?

I Wanda put a spell on you When Wanda is kidnapped, Maeve might need a little magic.

Brewing up Murder A witch, a murder, a dog...no, wait...a man..no...two men, three witches and a cat?

COOKING UP MURDER MYSTERY SERIES

Murder as Sticky as Jam Mona and Vicki are ready for the grand opening of Jammin' Honey until…their store goes up in smoke…

CHAPTER 1

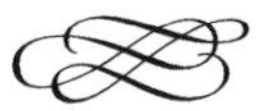

o Do:

1. Land new client.
2. Research the best baby-proofing system.
3. Sign up for prenatal exercise class?
4. Meet contractor who is doing garage reno.

I FROWNED AT THE BATTER IN THE KITCHENAID MIXER. WASN'T brownie batter supposed to be smooth and thin? Or was that just for brownies out of a box?

"Maybe I put in too much flour," I murmured, shifting my eight-month-old daughter Laurie on my hip. I glanced at the clock. The contractor we'd hired to do the garage renovation was swinging by in ten minutes to take a look at the space.

"Ma-ma," Laurie babbled, and my chest filled with happiness.

"That's the nicest thing anybody's ever called me, peanuty pie," I said, tapping her on the nose. Too late, I realized my finger was covered in flour, and now Laurie's nose had a dusty white streak.

"Whoops! Sorry, honey." I leaned toward the counter and reached for a napkin to dab her clean.

With a gurgle of glee, Laurie lurched forward, and I swiftly maneuvered to keep her from sailing out of my arms. "Now, listen—"

Laurie's tiny fingers curled around the edge of the half-empty flour jar, and time seemed to slow down as the plastic tub teetered on the edge of the countertop and tumbled into the air . . . and I couldn't do anything about it without losing my grip on Laurie. I watched in horror as it flipped upside-down, dumping a veritable mountain of flour. The jar hit the kitchen floor with a *thud,* belching a cloud of white powder into the air. Laurie giggled hysterically.

"What did you do, little miss? Now I have to clean that up before the contractor gets here." I glanced from the mess on the ground to Laurie and back again, running my free hand through my hair. Then I sighed and hurried to the storage closet for the broom, bouncing Laurie as we went. Despite the angst pinching my chest, I kept my voice calm. "Guess I need to move baby-proofing to the top of the list."

Humming, I grabbed the broom and stalked back to the flour-covered floor. Could I sweep one-handed?

Well, putting Laurie down was not an option. She'd beeline right into the mess.

I bent down to pick up the bin, and Laurie wiggled in my arms again, reaching toward the counter. Before I could see what she was grabbing, the open carton of eggs landed on the ground, the remaining three eggs oozing their yolks into the pile of white powder.

Laurie erupted into riotous giggles again, and I sucked in a deep breath to calm myself.

"Oh right. Real funny," I said to the little troublemaker in my arms. "How about you play with toys in the living room for a few minutes so I can get this cleaned up without any more mess?"

I glanced at the clock. Eight minutes. Gulping, I leaned the broom against the counter and speed-walked Laurie into the living room, setting her down next to a little yellow bus that sang the alphabet in a voice that sounded like a howling chipmunk. Super annoying, but it kept her engaged. Gritting my teeth, I pressed the button.

"A is for apple," yodeled the howling-chipmunk bus.

Laurie clapped her hands in delight. I hated that bus—Mom, of course, had bought it for Laurie over my protestations, saying it would help her learn to read—but Laurie loved it, and right now, I needed something to distract her.

"I love being a mom," I muttered as I stalked back to the kitchen to clean up the mess.

Seven minutes.

I turned the corner. Whiskers, our orange tabby kitten, was crouched in the middle of the floury mess, licking up the raw egg. Only she didn't look like an orange tabby anymore—everything except her face was white with flour, and eggs were smeared across her back. Had she . . . rolled in it?

I couldn't help it—I let out a shriek of frustration and despair. Whiskers froze, her eyes widening as she looked up at me. Then she darted past me, toward the carpeted living room. I reached out to grab her, but only managed to brush her fur before she wiggled under the living room couch. I balled my hands into fists. Even if I moved the couch, I wouldn't get her out of there until she was good and ready. There was a hole in the fabric underneath, and Whiskers had figured out how to climb inside the couch when she wanted a moment of peace from Laurie's grabby hands—or apparently when she knew she was in big trouble. I took in the trail of eggy sticky flour between the kitchen and couch, let a noise of desperation rise in my throat, and then returned to sweep up the mess.

I heard a car pull up outside, and panic lodged in my throat. Was the contractor here a couple of minutes early? I was still covered in flour! But maybe I could at least get the floor clean-ish before he came to the door?

As I dumped the last of the dry flour in the trash can and reached for a rag to mop up the last of the egg-and-flour concoction, I muttered, "Nice to meet you. Kate Connolly, private investigator, stay-at-home mom, and professional flour janitor."

And cat bather, I thought wryly, imagining Whiskers curled up in the belly of the couch. Could you get dried egg-flour out of the interior of a couch? Would it start to smell? The thought made me nauseated.

"This is what I get for trying to bake while holding an eight-month-old," I grumbled. *But I couldn't very well deny the twins brownies.* The worst of my food cravings were past me—I hoped—but being four and half months pregnant with twins certainly hadn't made me less hungry . . . or less interested in sugar.

I peered at the brownie batter. It really did look too thick. Had I put in too much flour?

What's the fix for that? Add milk?

The front door opened and closed, and Laurie squealed in delight.

"Hey hon!" called my husband, Jim.

Relief flooded me. Reinforcements were here. Now, I'd have help cleaning up and *eating* the brownies but not before meeting the contractor.

The contractor, Jo-Jo, still wasn't here.

I glanced at my phone and saw a text from him.

An emergency came up at the project I'm finishing. Can I come by tomorrow instead?

I slumped over the counter. I'd worked myself into a tizzy for nothing. At least I wouldn't have to meet the contractor looking like I'd fallen in a vat of flour.

"Jim!" I called. A moment later, Jim came into the kitchen, swinging Laurie in a circle.

He ground to a halt as soon as he saw me, his mouth twitching like he was trying to suppress a smirk. "Hey!" he said in a strangled voice.

"What is it?" I snapped, crossing my arms.

His composure broke, and he burst out laughing. "Honey, you're beautiful." He crossed the kitchen and planted a kiss on my lips. "But if I know you at all, you're going to want to wash your hair."

My hair? Horror filled me. I'd gotten flour on Laurie's nose . . . and then run my hand through my hair. I raced to the bathroom and looked in the mirror. Sure enough, a huge white streak ran straight down the middle, parting my hair like some sort of frizzy brown skunk.

"Watch Laurie!" I yelled as I slammed the door and turned on the shower.

Fifteen minutes later, I emerged from the bathroom with damp hair and a fresh change of clothes, feeling a bit more like myself. I found Jim and Laurie sitting on the living room couch, reading a book, and I gave Jim a real kiss.

"I'm sorry about that," I said, letting out a giggle as I thought back over the absurdity of the situation. "I was trying to bake and . . ."

"Decided to pioneer a hot new hair trend?" he asked with a devious grin.

"Definitely," I said, putting my hand on my hip and affecting the mannerisms of my always-fashionable best friend, Paula. "It's all the rage in Paris, you know."

"Seemed pretty sexy to me," he said, shooting me a wink. "But you're sexy no matter how you do your hair."

I rolled my eyes, but sank onto the couch and cuddled into his side. "You're silly."

He held up his free hand in mock affront. "I speak nothing but the truth."

"I need to start a prenatal exercise class." I glanced down at my baby bump. "I never got back into shape after Laurie, and I don't know how I'm going to reclaim my figure after having twins. And if you make one crack about cutting out baking and brownies, I'll knock you out flat."

Jim snorted. "Are you kidding? I value my life."

I chuckled.

"Anyway, you don't need to worry about that unless you want to. I love you the way you are. You're the momma!" he said firmly, putting down Laurie and pulling me into him for a bear hug. Laurie suddenly pressed the button on the infernal chipmunk bus

"A is for apple," screeched the bus.

"May I have this dance?" Jim asked, extending his hand to me.

Now it was my turn to burst out laughing. "What are you talking about?" I asked as I let him pull me to my feet and spin me around the room.

"I just got off the phone with Dave. You know he and his brothers bought that dance studio three or four years back?"

I nodded as Jim twirled me. "Yeah, I remember. What about it?" Dave had been Jim's best man at our wedding, and I'd always liked him and his brothers, Jack and Eddie. We hadn't seen them since much since Laurie was born—they'd been focused on running their business, and we'd been more than a little busy with Laurie and a string of homicide investigations I'd solved in my first months as a private investigator.

"Well"—we collapsed on the couch just as the chipmunk bus finished its song—"the studio's having some financial difficulty, and Dave called to invite us to attend a fundraiser. A public dance, you know, that they're hoping will bring in some money."

"Hold up! I'm four months pregnant and haven't danced in years."

"Come on," he said.

There was a knock, and before we could react, a key slipped into the latch and the door opened. My mom poked her head in. "Knock, knock!" she called.

"Hey!" said Jim.

Mom bounced into the room, holding up a shopping bag in triumph. No doubt something for Laurie that I'd absolutely hate. As long as it wasn't a clown, I'd tolerate it—I hoped Mom was past her clown phase.

"You have a theater degree," continued Jim. "It won't be hard to pick dancing back up. It's like riding a bike. Besides, I think we should take a set of dance lessons first. I'm sure they could use another couple of students. Help keep them afloat, you know?"

"Dance lessons?" cried Mom. She looked from Jim to me and back again with a huge smile on her face.

I groaned. I knew that look. It meant she was excited—and was about to make sure she got her way.

"Mom, don't—"

She scooped Laurie into her arms and spun her around the room. "We should all take dance lessons! You and Jim, and Galigani and me."

"But—"

"It will be so much fun!" she cried. "Besides, you need to get your exercise in, and it's not like you're about to pick jogging back up while you're pregnant with twins."

I bit my lip. She was right. Dancing was fun—certainly a lot more fun than squats, or whatever else they had pregnant moms do in prenatal fitness classes. And I wasn't as tired anymore now that I was in my second trimester. But I'd had such a complicated pregnancy, between being poisoned and in accidents and landing in the hospital. I wanted to keep the twins extra safe. "I don't know if I should be swung around that much," I said.

Mom waved away my objection. "Well, talk to Dr. Greene, of course. If she says you shouldn't do it, that's one thing. But you can't dismiss the idea without even asking her."

"Besides," said Jim "there's one other thing I haven't told you yet."

"What?" I asked, crossing my arms.

"Dave said there have been some weird things happening at the studio. Someone cut a hole in the roof in the middle of the night, and it sounded like a few things have gone missing. Plus, a dead bird showed up on the dance floor right before a group class was about to start. Weird, right?"

Now *that* was interesting. I leaned forward. "What sorts of things are missing?"

Jim grinned. He knew me too well—at the mention of something mysterious, I was hooked. "He didn't say, exactly. And maybe it's all a coincidence, but I know I'm married to San Francisco's most attractive *and* most talented private investigator, and I thought you might want to poke around a little. See if there's anyone who might be trying to sabotage my best friend's business. What do you say? Can I hire you? Where do I sign?"

I slouched back against the couch cushions and held up my hands in surrender. "Fine, we can take dance lessons. I don't have a client right now, and I could use a little mystery. It'll keep me from trying to bake again, at least."

Mom squealed in delight, dancing Laurie around the room again.

"I'll call and get the lesson set up," Jim said, jumping up. "We'll take the lessons slow, I promise. And maybe we can help them throw the fundraiser too?"

"Sure," I answered. "Let me call Dr. Greene to ask if the lessons are safe, but let's definitely help Dave throw the fundraiser. That'll give me a good excuse to spend time at the studio looking for anything suspicious. Maybe Paula will help too. I'll text her. Oh, and the contractor said something came up. He's coming tomorrow to look at the garage."

With the price of real estate in San Francisco, we'd decided to convert our garage into a bedroom for the twins, rather than look for a house that would accommodate our growing family. And I couldn't wait to get started.

I reached for my phone to dial Dr. Greene just as a streak of white and orange barreled out from under the couch, leaving a trail of flour in its wake.

"Whiskers!" I bolted to my feet and chased after the kitten. "Get your tail back here!"

CHAPTER 2

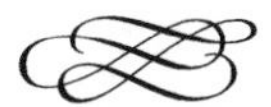

o Do:

1. Research best baby-proofing system.
2. Land new client? (Maybe Dave's studio?)
3. Dance lesson—tonight.
4. Meet contractor who is doing garage reno.

"MRS. CONNOLLY?"

I surveyed the fiery-haired man standing on my doorstep. He had thick glasses, a bulbous nose, and so much energy that he couldn't seem to keep his hands still. I glanced toward the street. A pickup truck bearing the name *Jo-Jo's Jobs* was parked at the curb, but this couldn't possibly be the contractor, could it?

"Yes, I'm Kate Connolly," I said, trying to hide my amusement. "And you are?"

His head bobbed like a pigeon, and he grabbed my hand and shook it. "Jo-Jo Jones," he exclaimed in a strong Irish brogue. "I'm here to do the garage renovation job."

"Of course," I said, drawing back my hand and glancing at my watch. He was an hour early, and Jim wasn't home yet. But better early than late, right? At least I hadn't tried to bake anything today. I beckoned him inside. "Come on in."

He stayed on the porch and waved a sheaf of papers at me with frenetic energy. "I got muddy boots, lassie. Don't wanna track it in yer house. Got yer plans here and just need to take a look around, make sure everything's in order here to start. So, maybe if you'd just open up the garage door, I could go in and outta there?"

"Oh, sure! I'll do that," I said. I closed the door and opened up the garage for him. As the door began to roll up, I called, "Just let me know if you need anything!"

Jo-Jo had as much energy as my mom. *Well. Paula did say he was eccentric.*

And also, that he did great work at half the cost of the big general contracting companies in the area.

I could live with eccentric.

At a little cry from Laurie's room, I padded down the hall and into her ducky-themed nursery, accented with pink and mint green, and scooped her out of her crib.

"Hello, little duck," I whispered, smacking a big kiss on her cheek. "How is my favorite girl?"

A meticulously clean Whiskers rubbed up against my legs. The evening before, I'd bathed all the flour and crusted egg off Whiskers while my mom vacuumed the living room and finished the brownies. They'd tasted more like cookies than brownies, but they were still delicious if I did say so myself.

Hard to go wrong with chocolate and sugar.

In the living room, I set Laurie down next to the coffee table and sat beside her. "Guess what, peanut? You get to see Mr. Kenny today while Mama and Daddy and Grandma go to dance class!"

Dr. Greene had assured me that dancing was a perfectly good prenatal exercise, as long as I avoided full-on acrobatics. I assured her that I had no intention of letting Jim, or anyone, toss me into the air, and so dance lessons were on—starting tonight.

And so was a little sleuthing.

Laurie's squeal interrupted my reverie. She reached up and

gripped the edge of the coffee table as I made a silly face at her. "That's right," I said. "You're going to have a lot of fun with Mr. Kenny!"

My phone buzzed, and I opened a text from Paula.

Let's do it!! I'm between clients and need to do something besides laundry and changing diapers, stat.

I pumped my fist. Paula's savvy interior design skills would be a huge help with the fundraiser, and I wanted an excuse to spend more time with her.

Tell me about it, I typed back. *You would not believe the mess Laurie and Whiskers made yesterday.*

The phone buzzed with her reply: *Wait till there's 5 of them.*

My nose scrunched, and I typed back. *5?*

L, twin 1, twin 2, cat, Jim, she replied.

I snorted and searched my mind for a witty reply, then glanced at Laurie and gasped.

My baby was standing, clinging to the edge of the coffee table. She'd pulled herself to her feet.

My. Baby. Had. Pulled. Herself. To. Her Feet.

I dropped the phone and squealed, "Good job, peanut!"

Laurie fell back onto her bottom, looking almost affronted, like she couldn't figure out how she'd ended up back where she'd started.

"You did so good!" I picked up my phone and opened the camera app in case she did it again. "You stood up!"

Laurie, Prodigy Baby Extraordinaire and no doubt future partner in *Connolly and Connolly Private Investigators,* gurgled and clapped.

A pounding at the basement door which separated our house and garage interrupted my celebration. Must be Jo-Jo. I grabbed the $10,000 cashier's check off the counter.

Farewell, life savings.

I opened the door to the garage to find Jo-Jo jumping up and down. "Mrs. Connolly!" he yelled in that thick Irish brogue. "It's grand!"

"What's grand?" I asked slowly.

"The project!"

He paced the garage back and forth, his flaming hair taking on a life of its own, as if it too, thought our garage-turned-bedroom reno was *grand*.

"I'm glad you think so," I said, crossing my arms and taking a step into the garage, then closing the door behind me so Whiskers couldn't make a mad dash for the great outdoors. Eccentric, indeed.

No, he didn't have *as much* energy as my mom—he had *more* energy than my mom. *Paula will certainly never hear the end of this.*

"Everything's set to begin." He held his arms up like a referee declaring a 49ers touchdown.

"No trouble with the plans, then? You'll be able to do it for the price you quoted?"

"No trouble at all! It'll be under budget! Gonna be a grand addition, lassie. I'll begin the work soon!"

"Wonderful!" I held out the cashier's check. "I guess I owe you this, then."

He took the check from me and stuffed it into his breast pocket. "There's just one more thing, lassie. But not to worry." His voice hesitated but his feet didn't. He kept up his rapid pacing. It was making me dizzy. "I'm not sure exactly what day I'll be set to start. I 'ave to catch a flight back to Dublin tomorrow to get me visa straightened right out."

I tried to process what he'd just said. "You're leaving the country tomo—"

He ran into a pile of cardboard boxes and sent half of them tumbling to the floor, stirring up a layer of dust. My throat tickled, and I sneezed.

When I opened my eyes again, he was already out the garage and in my driveway, waving back at me. "We'll get ya started as soon as I'm back, lassie!"

He practically waltzed to his truck, clambered into the cab, and drove off, his tires screeching. I stared after him, my brain still trying to catch up with that one unexpected, terrifying detail.

Wait! What?

What did *getting his visa straightened out* entail? What if they didn't let him back in the country, and I'd just sent him away with a cashier's check for ten thousand dollars? My throat felt tight. But he'd already driven away. I couldn't change it now.

I could only hope that Paula hadn't steered us wrong and that Jo-Jo wasn't running off with our deposit.

I tiptoed into the living room to check on Laurie. She was chewing contentedly on the foot of a stuffed duck. All was well in babyland. I collapsed onto the couch and rested a hand on my midsection.

We were going to think positively about this.

Jo-Jo would come back. And my biggest problem was going to be dealing with all that frenzied energy. If Jo-Jo and Mom worked together, I was pretty sure they could singlehandedly power the sun.

I'm an extrovert, but this might feel like a very long renovation. "It'll be worth it for you two," I murmured to the twins, still cradling my bump. "We'll have a beautiful nursery."

Snagging my phone, I fired off one more text to Paula: *He's going back to Ireland tomorrow?*

* * *

KENNY ARRIVED JUST AS I FINISHED PUTTING ON MY MASCARA.

"Kate, can I order—"

"Pizza money is on the counter," I said with a grin. Kenny, who'd just turned eighteen, lived to raid our fridge and to devour any pizza we would buy him. His folks still hadn't given up trying to make him a vegan.

He flipped his pink hair—the tips used to be purple but now they were blue— and gave me two thumbs up before scooping up Laurie.

I stared at his hair. The tips were blue on *one* side, but on the other . . . "Did you shave half your head?"

He groaned. "Don't remind me."

Blinking a few times, I asked, "*Why* did you shave half your head? I mean, it looks great—edgy and artistic, and all that. But you don't seem happy about it."

"I got a bird stuck in it," he mumbled.

"You got a *what* stuck in it?"

He sat down with Laurie and started to play peek-a-boo. "So, I took Siena—you know, the one with the nose ring—on a date to the zoo."

Ah, yes, Kenny had been quite enthusiastic about Nose Ring, as I'd taken to calling her in my head. He'd met her a couple of weeks ago while busking with his tuba at Fisherman's Wharf.

He covered his eyes. "We went into the aviary. Peekaboo!" He opened his hands and peeked out at Laurie.

"Oh no." I grimaced.

"Oh yes." He covered his eyes again. "Anyway, we were walking through the South American Rainforest Aviary exhibit, and there was this obnoxious fly buzzing around me. I don't know if it thought my hair was a pink fruit or a flower or what. And this green jay absolutely divebombed the heck out of that fly."

I tried not to laugh. "That's horrible."

"Darn bird collided with me and got its claws all tangled in my hair. I couldn't get it out, Siena couldn't get it out, the zookeeper chick couldn't get it out, zookeeper chick's manager couldn't get it out." He was still covering his eyes, and Laurie reached up and pulled his hand off his face. "The only way to free the bird without hurting it was to cut it out of my hair. So, instead of cutting all my hair short to match or walking around with a weird mangled spot, I just shaved that side."

"Did you get another date out of it, at least?" I asked sympathetically, pursing my lips to force myself to maintain a serious expression.

"Eh, there wasn't really that X-factor, you know? Even before the bird incident. I don't think either of us was really feeling it. But I did get zookeeper chick's phone number."

Jim emerged from the bedroom, looking handsome in his button-up and slacks. I glanced down at my jeans and plain blue maternity blouse and wondered if I was underdressed.

"Can you teach Laurie how to play the tuba tonight?" Jim asked. "Maybe get her a spot playing for the symphony?"

"Sure thing," Kenny said with a smirk. "We'll audition together next month."

"Enjoy the pizza!" I said, slinging my purse over my shoulder. "Try to leave me a slice. I'm eating for three."

"No promises. Enjoy the dance class!"

"Wish me luck—I hear that some weird things have been happening at the studio, and I'm hoping I can solve the mystery for them."

"Let me know if I can help you track down the bad guy," called Kenny. "Those stories always play well with girls." He carried Laurie over to that awful chipmunk bus and said, "Should we work on your alphabet, Miss L?"

It was only a twelve-minute drive to *Tre Fratelli Danzanti,* which was nestled in the Mission District right between a Mexican food restaurant and another dance studio. We lucked into finding a parking spot right away—pulling up just as someone else was leaving.

"Excellent," I said to Jim as I climbed out of the car. "That'll give us some time to talk to Dave and his brothers before class."

Mom had texted to say she and Galigani weren't coming tonight, so it would be a private lesson for Jim and me.

Jim slid his credit card into the parking meter, then nudged me in the ribs and looped my arm through his. "Just in case they're in need of San Francisco's finest private investigator?"

I smiled innocently. "Well, I can't wait to hear more about the weird things happening at the studio and I couldn't very well turn down a friend in need."

The lobby of the dance studio was clean but nondescript, with a simple oak desk and computer, plus a few chairs. The only thing that stood out was the quote stenciled on the wall behind the desk: *Dance first. Think later. It's the natural order. -Samuel Beckett (sort of)*

I pointed at it, and Jim snorted. "Typical Dave."

A woman in her late twenties came around the corner, her floral minidress swishing over a pair of pink leggings. "Oh!" she cried, her hand flying to the flower in her curly black hair. "You must be Jim and Kate!"

"Yes," I said. "Are you our dance teacher?"

She crossed to us and took both my hands in hers. "I'm Petunia Petal, Dave's girlfriend. He's told me so much about you—I recognized you from your pictures."

I tried my hardest to keep my expression neutral, but she must have seen a look of amusement flash across my face, because she laughed and added in a conspiratorial whisper, "Well, really I'm Mary Williams, but don't tell anyone. I go by Petunia Petal with everyone in the dance world. I'm breaking into doing it professionally—dancing, not just teaching—and it's easier to be memorable with a flashy stage name. There are too many Mary Williamses in the world for anyone to find me by Googling."

"Great to meet you, Petunia," said Jim.

Just then, Dave came barreling toward us from the back. "Jim! Kate!"

Dave, the oldest of the *Tre Fratelli Danzanti* - three dancing brothers -was tall, dark and Italian, a fine handsome catch considering that alone, but the fact he could dance would make any girl swoon. He hugged Jim, thumping him on the back.

"Been too long," said Jim.

"It has been." Dave slung his arm around Petunia. "Hon, this is my best friend Jim and his wife, Kate. Jim and Kate, meet . . . Petunia?" He glanced at her with a questioning expression.

"Embarrassing to forget your girlfriend's name," I quipped.

He blushed. "Well, it's just—"

"She told us," I said warmly. "Mary sometimes, but Petunia at the studio."

Dave gave us a smile and a wink. "In that case, this is my girlfriend Petunia. She dances professionally and also teaches classes here." He turned to Petunia. "Jim's an ad guru, and Kate manages an architectural firm office."

"Not anymore!" I shook my head. "I left the soul-sucking corporate world behind when Laurie was born."

"Good for you," said Petunia. "Are you staying at home with her, then?"

"Kate's the best private investigator in town." Jim rested his hands on my shoulders. "She's been solving homicides left and right."

Dave's jaw dropped. "Whoa, that's awesome!"

My chest swelled with pride.

We chatted about my most recent case for a few minutes, and just when I was hoping they'd talk about the mysterious incidents at the studio, Dave changed the subject.

"Thanks for signing up for the lesson, by the way," he said, shifting uncomfortably. "When we talked, I wasn't trying to get you to spend money propping us up—"

No need for him to feel uncomfortable. "I jumped at the opportunity," I interjected. "I'd been meaning to sign up for an exercise class, and this sounded like fun."

Dave visibly relaxed.

"Tell us about this fundraiser," said Jim. "Is the studio in trouble?"

"Oh, it's not for the studio," said Dave, beckoning us toward the hall. We followed him to a brightly lit room with a gleaming wooden dance floor and a wall of mirrors. A divider on one side partitioned it off from the next room over. "I mean, the studio makes a profit, but not enough of a profit to pay us owners much. That's fine for me and Eddie, but Jack, well . . ."

Petunia's face softened, and she whispered, "Jack and Sharon have been trying to have a baby for five years."

Instinctively, I cradled my baby bump. "Sharon's a kindergarten teacher, isn't she?"

"First grade," said Dave, his lips set in a grim line. "She's desperate for a baby, and . . . I'm pretty sure they wouldn't mind me telling you this—their insurance doesn't cover any fertility treatments, and they can't afford them on her salary and his earnings from the studio."

"Oh," I whispered. My heart went out to Sharon. She'd always seemed so warm and maternal.

"Anyway." Dave scuffed a toe on the gleaming wooden floor. "They've scrimped and saved, and our folks pitched in, but they're still about $3000 short. We're trying to raise some money to give Jack a $3000 bonus, and we figured we'd do a 1950s swing dance. Between the cover charge, some money we can make from the cash bar, and the extra lessons people will sign up for . . ."

"Can we help?" I asked. "My friend Paula—you remember Paula, right? She was my maid of honor. She's incredible at interior design. And Jim can do posters and marketing! And I can help where you need me."

Like figuring out about those weird things happening at the studio, I thought.

Dave's face lit up, and he glanced at Jim. "That'd be incredible. Do you have time to design posters for us? I know you're working with some big-time clients these days, and I'd hate to impose."

"I absolutely have time," Jim said firmly. He glanced at his watch. "Hey, there's still five minutes before the lesson is scheduled to start. Let's get all the information together, and I'll work up a draft poster for you tomorrow."

Dave thumped him on the back. "You're a good man. I have a whole plan on the computer. Let's go print it out."

The guys left for the lobby, leaving Petunia and me on the dance floor. "Oh, I'm so glad they gave us a moment," said Petunia in another one of her conspiratorial whispers. "I've been *dying* to ask you a question."

Here we go. Why yes, I'd be happy to investigate for you. No charge. Thank you for asking.

She half-covered her mouth to hide her sheepish grin. "You've known Dave for years. Do you have any ideas on how I can get him to propose?"

CHAPTER 3

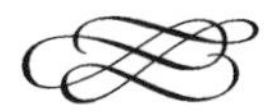

Petunia wants to marry Dave?

"Oh," I said, momentarily confused. "How long have you been dating?"

She glanced down at the floor and bit her lip. "A year. I know that doesn't sound like very long, but I'm about to turn thirty, and I really want kids, and . . . I let my last boyfriend string me along for five years before I accepted that he was never going to commit."

"I'm sorry."

"I don't need him to propose right away." She looked up and met my gaze. "Although I'd be thrilled if he did. I love him. I'm *in* love with him." A giddy smile flashed across her face. "I just need to know that he's eventually going to commit, you know? That history isn't going to repeat itself."

"Have you talked to Dave about your feelings?" I asked.

"I think so. Maybe I should have said it more directly—"

"Petunia, darling," said an older gentleman from the doorway. "How are you?"

Older or not, his British accent and neatly pressed suit no doubt made most women swoon. I glanced down at my jeans. *Yup. Definitely underdressed.*

"That's Leo," said Petunia, smoothing her floral skirt. "He's the dance instructor for your lesson." She shifted from foot to foot and whispered, "I'm sorry. I feel like I shouldn't have asked you. You won't tell Dave, will you? I don't want him to feel pressured into something he isn't ready for."

I promised I wouldn't breathe a word, and a moment later, Jim returned.

"I'll leave you to it," called Petunia, fleeing the room.

I glanced at the clock. Five p.m. *Time to dance.* I took Jim's hand.

Leo studied us, his eyes landing for an extra beat on my visible baby bump. "Have you danced before?" he asked, each word crisp.

"Mostly musical theater stuff," I gave him my best jazz hands, and he looked suitably unimpressed.

He turned to Jim.

Jim grimaced. "A little, I mean, you know we waltzed for our wedding."

"Very well. Let's start with a simple rock step. Like this." He demonstrated for Jim. "Step with your left for two counts, step with your right for two counts, step back for one count—no, with your left foot—step forward for one count. One, two, three, four, five, six—no, other foot. Smaller steps, now. There we go."

After a half dozen tries, Jim managed a passable rock step. His rhythm was shaky, but the steps were in the right order. I cheered aloud.

Leo smirked at my antics. "Now, for the women's part—"

"I know how to rock step," I said, demonstrating.

Leo's bushy eyebrows drew together, but he smiled. "A natural! Very well. Why don't you try it together? We'll start in open position . . . hands like this."

Jim and I clasped fingers in front of us, facing each other directly, and Leo began to count, "One, two . . ."

I tuned him out. *Step, step, rock step . . .*

As Jim and I stepped toward each other, my eyes widened in alarm. I lost my balance, tipping forward and falling straight at Jim. My right foot shot backward and my arms flailed as I tried to steady myself. Jim caught me in his strong arms just as I let out a shriek. He righted me back on my feet, and I stammered, "What happened?"

Leo pinched the bridge of his nose.

"I do know how to rock step!" I hurried to explain. Tipping over would have been mortifying to begin with, but tipping over right after I'd assured him I knew what I was doing? My cheeks felt red hot. "It's just . . . it felt different. I'm pregnant with twins, and the extra weight threw me off. I just have to account for that."

And my abs are weak! Goodness, how did they get so weak?

"Of course you do, hon," Jim said, resting a comforting hand on my lower back.

"Mmm-hmm." Leo pursed his lips. "Perhaps we should start from the beginning for you as well."

I stiffened my back. "Let's run it again. I won't fall this time."

"Right-o, then. One, two, three, four, five, six . . ."

Step, step, rock step. Victory! True to my word, I put all of my focus on my balance and didn't fall. The rock step was a bit clunky—not my finest work—but I tilted my chin at Leo in triumph.

So there!

Leo's face remained fastidiously neutral.

Jim and I rock-stepped several more times, and then Leo said, "Now, let's turn the single steps into triple steps. Like this. Let's do the women's part first." He showed me how to triple step, and I didn't bother to tell him I already knew how.

"Ready?" he asked in that pristine British accent.

I nodded mutely.

He clapped his hands. "Go on, then. Rock step, tri-ple step, tri-ple step."

I kept my balance on the rock step, but as I finished the second triple step, I felt a flash of horror. I was tipping forward . . . nothing to be done . . . Leo's quietly horrified face flashed before my eyes just as Jim caught me again.

"Ahem," said Leo, "so, we'll want to work on your center of gravity."

I was sure I was blushing furiously, but I just said, "Let's run it again. I think I know where I went wrong."

This time I focused on nothing but my balance, making sure to lean back just a little on the transition to the second triple step. It wasn't my best dance move of all time, but at least I didn't humiliate myself.

Leo clicked his tongue. "That'll do. Jim, why don't you try? For your part, you're mirroring Kate's movement, so you'll want to step back with your left foot . . ."

Jim stepped back with his right foot.

"*Left* foot," said Leo, enunciating each word.

Jim stepped back with his left foot, and Leo broke down the triple step movement by movement.

Jim gave it his most valiant effort but got tangled in his own feet.

"Alright, here's where you went wrong," said Leo.

Jim gave it another try and stumbled when he tried to triple-step forward on the wrong foot. Three attempts in a row.

Leo sighed and massaged his temples. "Alright, why don't we try it this way?"

Finally, Jim got the steps in the right order. I high-fived him, but Leo muttered under his breath, "And yet no rhythm or musicality in sight."

Jim laughed, totally unruffled, but annoyance flared in my chest. Jim was working hard! There was no need for Leo to be sarcastic. He knew Jim was a beginner.

"Run it again," said Leo.

Jim took a triple step backward when he was supposed to rock-step. He threw his hands out wide. "I am the worst," he called. "I'm sorry. I did that wrong."

"Well, the customer is always right," muttered Leo.

Maybe there *was* a mystery here at the dance studio—the mystery of why Leo was such a pill.

I snapped, "Now look here—"

Angry shouts from the lobby cut me off. *No, not just angry—enraged. Viscerally enraged.*

Jim and I glanced at each other in confusion, and then Jim darted for the door. I followed, my heart hammering. We burst into the lobby to see a short, balding man letting loose a string of epithets. Petunia stood behind the desk staring him down.

"Dammit, woman, let me talk to the owners!" he screamed, a vein bulging in his forehead.

Petunia didn't say a word in response.

I sensed movement behind me, and then two men ran past us. *Dave and . . . no, Jack and Eddie.*

Eddie planted himself in front of Balding Man, his arms crossed, and Jack stood alongside the desk.

Balding Man fell into glowering silence.

"Get out of here, Monte," hissed Petunia. "You know they're not selling."

"Oh yeah?" Monte demanded. "I don't think you speak for them, cupcake."

I bristled and stepped forward, about to give this idiot a piece of my mind, but Eddie said calmly, "You'll walk out that door in the next three seconds, or I'll call the police and have you arrested for trespassing."

At the mention of the police, some of Monte's bluster faded. He took a step back.

"You'll sell," he spat. "You'll see. Just you wait. You're gonna be so miserable you'll want to *pay* me to take this crap hole off your hands."

"Now what's that supposed to mean?" Petunia put her hands on her hips.

"I said, get out," Eddie growled. "I won't say it again."

Monte flipped him the bird, then turned and stalked out of the studio.

"Unpleasant business," muttered a British accent from behind me, and I realized Leo had followed us out.

"Yes, very unpleasant," replied Eddie, scowling in the direction of the door. Then he turned to us, brightening. "Jim and Kate! Dave said you were coming."

"Where is Dave?" Jim asked, wrinkling his nose.

Petunia typed something on the computer and said, "He went out to grab some subs for dinner. Monte's a coward, and Dave intimidates him. He must have been watching the studio, so he could come bother us as soon as Dave left."

This was my opportunity. "What's been going on with Monte? I take it this isn't your first run-in."

Jim shifted beside me, and I could tell he was trying to suppress a smirk. He could see right through me.

Jack, who was shorter than Eddie and Dave by a full head but looked remarkably like Dave, slumped into one of the lobby chairs. "Monte opened up a dance studio next door, and he wants our space."

"Wants to drive out the competition, more like," muttered Petunia, re-tucking the flower in her hair. "Our dance instructors are better than his."

Jim stepped over to the window and peered out, no doubt looking to see if Monte was still lurking. "Why would someone open up a dance studio right next to the competition?" he asked, still staring outside. "Doesn't seem like a winning strategy for a successful business."

Eddie rolled his eyes. "It's not, but—"

Dave walked in, cheerily holding up a bag of subs. He stopped short, his eyes darting from his brothers to Petunia to Jim and me. "What happened?" he demanded.

"Monte paid us a visit," said a tight-lipped Petunia. She rubbed her temples. "Gave all of us quite the headache."

"Is there anything I can do to help?" I asked, taking a step forward. If there was ever a time to offer my PI services . . .

But Dave waved me off. "You guys are already doing so much for us. We'll deal with Monte. He's more of an annoyance than anything."

The door jangled, and a crew of giggling girls walked in, with an equal number of much-less-enthusiastic guys following in their wake. Late high school or early college, I thought, and no doubt the guys had been dragged here.

"Uncle Leo!" squealed one of the girls.

I glanced at Leo, and he looked almost softhearted. "Ready for the lesson, then, love?" He trained a steely glare on a boy with moppish blond hair. "You'll not drop my favorite niece on any of the lifts this week, mind you."

There was the grumpy, impatient Leo we'd met on the dance floor.

I looked at the clock and realized that our hour was up—this group must be Leo's next lesson.

Jim and I excused ourselves and headed off to finish the evening at our favorite Italian pizzeria. Tony, the perennially tall, dark, and handsome son of the restauranteur, greeted us and showed us to our table. Only when we sat down, did I realize how famished I was. All that exercise made the babies hungry.

"Monte was odd," Jim said as I scanned the menu to decide if I should add a second appetizer to our usual order.

"Leo was odd," I grumbled.

At that, Jim laughed aloud, then reached out and grabbed my hand. "You figured out your balance beautifully. You're a natural dancer. It's just going to take a little practice on each move to figure out what *balance* looks like with the twins jostling for space. And I'll . . . well, I'll get the hang of it eventually."

Tony took our order—I stuck to our usual bruschetta for the appetizer—and then my phone buzzed.

It was a text from Kenny.

Laurie is fast asleep and already an expert at the tuba.

I showed the text to Jim. "I'm so grateful for Kenny. You really hit it out of the park when you asked him to be our regular babysitter. He thoughtful, dependable—"

The phone vibrated with another text from Kenny. *Any chance you could pick up ice cream on your way back?*

"—and dependably starving." Jim finished my sentence with a chuckle and leaned across the table to kiss me.

* * *

"Jo-Jo can be eccentric," said Paula as the waiter set down our hot drinks at brunch that Saturday. "Always enthusiastic. Occasionally forgetful. Make sure you write down everything he needs to remember. But I am *certain* he won't run off with your ten thousand dollars."

"I hope so." I buried my face in my hands. "If we lose that money, we won't be able to afford a new contractor, and we won't have a nursery for the twins, and I'll have to take apart Laurie's nursery to bunk all three of them in there, and move my office onto the kitchen table."

"You already do almost all of your work at the kitchen table," Paula pointed out. "I don't even know why you have an office in there."

I gave a strangled cry and curled my fingers around my steaming coffee cup. It was a little chilly at our outdoor table.

"But," she hastily added, "it doesn't matter. Jo-Jo *will* come back and finish the work. You won't lose that money."

Please let Paula be right, I prayed fervently.

Mom slumped into the seat next to Paula. "Albert won't take dance lessons with me! It was excuse after excuse."

"Well," I said, taking a sip of decaf, "as my mother, you're contractually obligated to keep dating him until I get my PI license."

Albert Galigani, my mom's boyfriend, was also the licensed PI who was supervising me while I worked toward my six thousand hours of experience that would let me get my own license. We defined "supervision" loosely, but he'd been an invaluable mentor and I loved him dearly.

Mom rolled her eyes dramatically and motioned for the waiter. "A pot of tea, please!" Then she turned back to Paula and me. "'I'm not good at dancing,'" she said in a spot-on mimicry of Galigani. "Well"—she popped back into her normal histrionic voice—"that's why you take lessons, my dear. 'What if I break my ankle again?' Perhaps dancing would strengthen your ankle! 'Too much exercise.' You know your doctor wants you to exercise more. It's good for your heart. 'I hate music.' *Objectively* a lie. He loves music, and he knows I know it."

Leave it to Mom for a dramatic reenactment. I'd gotten my artistic chops from her.

"Well," I said in a teasing voice, "maybe you'd like Dave's brother Eddie better. He's still single, and an excellent dancer."

"Still single, eh? I always liked Eddie. Maybe I should get myself a younger man," warbled Mom with a wink, mollified for the moment.

Paula pulled a fussy Chloe out of the stroller parked between her chair and Mom's. "Kate says there's also an odious teacher named Leo. He's the worst, but he does have a British accent, so he can't be the *very* worst."

I wrinkled my nose. "Ah, yes. Leo. He's closer to your age, but he teaches dance, so I imagine he wouldn't claim to hate music."

Paula tucked Chloe under a nursing cover, and I felt a little pang of nostalgia. Laurie was already getting so big—we'd left Laurie, along with Paula's two-year-old son, with Kenny for the afternoon—and I missed her being that tiny.

Instinctively, I cradled my baby bump, the nostalgia vanishing into a flare of panic. Laurie was getting bigger, but soon enough I'd have *two* teeny-tiny babies and a one-year-old capable of opening drawers and dumping flour on the floor. *Imagine the chaos . . .*

Batting away the panic, I blurted, "The money the event raises is going to cover fertility treatments for Dave's sister-in-law. She and Jack have been trying to get pregnant for five years."

Paula's eyes widened, and she sat up straighter. "You didn't tell me that."

"I didn't know until last night."

"Poor thing," said Mom as the waiter set a white teapot full of hot water and a basket of tea bags in front of her. She sorted through the selection and plucked out a bag of Earl Grey. I looked mournfully at my decaf and asked the waiter if I could have a pot of tea too.

He nodded brusquely, and swept back toward the kitchen.

"Well"—Paula's eyes were alight—"this is about more than building my business and having something to do. We're going to make this the best fundraiser of all time." She grabbed a legal pad out of the stroller and started scribbling line items. "Can we run by the studio after this, so I can take a look at the space?"

"Vera!" called a man's familiar voice.

I froze, and even Mom looked startled.

Hank, Mom's ex-boyfriend, was walking toward our table.

CHAPTER 4

Maybe *ex-boyfriend* wasn't quite the right word. Mom and Hank hadn't ever properly broken up. Come to think of it, they hadn't ever properly been a couple. She'd casually dated both Hank and Galigani for a few months, and she and Galigani had become exclusive by default when Hank had gone abroad for some extensive traveling with his daughter.

"Isn't he in Europe?" whispered Paula.

"Apparently not anymore," I murmured.

It wasn't that there was anything wrong with Hank. He was a great guy. I just really didn't want anything to come between my mom and Galigani because Galigani was a friend and crazy about her.

The waiter brought me my own teapot, and I dunked an Earl Grey tea bag in the hot water, enjoying the spicy scent of bergamot.

Mom stood up and gave Hank a quick hug.

He pecked her on the cheek. "It's so good to see you."

"Please, sit down," Mom said, nearly stammering.

Paula and I looked at each other with matching expressions of consternation. Mom was rarely flustered.

Hank took the seat next to me, and said, "Kate, I may have a case for you to solve."

I sat up, suddenly interested despite my trepidation about his reappearance in our lives. "Oh?"

He grinned at my mom. "Your mother is looking more beautiful than ever, and we should figure out the source of her eternal youth."

Mom giggled—positively giggled! "Hank, you sly thing."

"I aim to please." He winked.

The waiter approached and asked if Hank wanted anything to drink, but Hank waved him off. "Just stopping to say hello," he said by way of explanation. "Kate, how's that baby of yours doing?"

"Oh!" Mom picked up her phone and opened a recent picture of Laurie—one of my favorites. It showed Laurie sitting with Whiskers in her lap, with a huge grin on Laurie's face as she looked down at the kitten. "You've got to see how she's grown."

"Well, isn't she just the cutest little thing?" said Hank. He nodded at Paula. "We've met before. What was your name again?"

Paula looked up from her notepad, where she'd resumed her furious scribbling. "Oh, I'm Paula, Kate's best friend. Hank, right?"

Hank nodded and shuffled a hand through his close-cropped beard. "Whatcha working on over there that's so fascinating, Miss Paula?"

Mom, who seemed to have recovered herself at last, said, "Paula is a world-class interior designer, and she's agreed to help out Kate and Jim's friends throw a benefit dance. Well, we're all helping, but Paula is going to make it look spectacular."

"Oh, what kind of benefit dance?"

Too late, I remembered that Hank and Mom had once taken salsa dance classes together. Which meant . . .

"A 1950s swing dance!" said Paula. "Jim and Kate are taking lessons at *Tre Fratelli Danzanti*, and Vera was going to take classes, too, but she's short a partner."

I glared murder at Paula. My mom was *not* short a partner, she just . . . had one who didn't want to dance.

"Oh, *Tre Fratelli Danzanti*? I've been there a few times. What do you say, Vera? Should we put on our dancing shoes again?"

I bit down hard on my lip to keep from audibly sighing. *Were* Galigani and my mom even exclusive? She wasn't seeing anyone else, but it wasn't like I was privy to their closest conversations. I wasn't *really* sure how serious they were. Although it sure seemed like they were fast on their way to falling in love.

Hank bantered about the fundraiser with Paula and Mom, and by the time he left, Mom had decided she'd make some 1950s-themed food for the event, if it was all right with Petunia and Dave. I was everyone's executive assistant—I'd help Jim with marketing, Paula with interior decorating, and my mom with food.

Even as I took copious notes, my thoughts drifted back to the hole in the roof, the dead bird, and Monte's strange threats.

And maybe, just maybe, I'd have time to solve the odd happenings at the studio. At least *this* mystery didn't come with a side of murder.

* * *

MONDAY ROLLED AROUND, AND JO-JO APPEARED ON OUR DOORSTEP, bright red hair wreathing his face like a flaming geyser. I'd never been so relieved to see anyone. *The ten thousand dollar man!*

"Everything work out with your visa?" I asked, shifting Laurie to my other hip.

"Visa's taken care of, and I got ta spend a bit of time with me aunts and uncles and cousins in Cork," he said in that thick Irish brogue, his head bobbing rhythmically. "And I'll get yer reno started today. It'll be the grandest I've ever done!"

I opened the garage door for him and then sat at the dining room table to hold Laurie while online-ordering a few things for the benefit.

Laurie was having an extra-squirmy day, and I caught her arm right before she helped herself to my open Sharpie.

"Not for babies," I sang as I capped it—and set it out of reach for good measure.

She flailed, so I set her down on the ground next to me.

"Need to get out your wiggles?" I cooed. "You have so many wiggles!"

She clapped.

"So many wiggles!" I turned my attention back to the screen and, out of curiosity, looked up Monte's dance studio, Dare to Dance. It looked pretty normal—similar to *Tre Fratelli Danzanti*. Nothing on the website screamed *would leave a dead bird on a competitor's dance floor*.

I pulled his last name—Vander—and logged into the background check database with Galigani's credentials.

"Monte Vander," I murmured. "On his second marriage, no arrest history." Nothing stood out there, either.

A tiny hand patted my leg. I looked down, and Laurie had pulled herself to her feet again. "Good job, little duck!" I squealed.

My computer dinged, and I opened a new email from Jim—a marketing poster to look over. I double-clicked the file, and then a text came in from a number I didn't recognize.

Kate! It's Petunia. Did Jim tell you about the break-in and bird? I know Dave mentioned it to him on the phone.

My heart pounded. I was in business.

Yes, I texted back. *Can I help?*

A few seconds passed, and then she sent me a photo. *This was on the front desk when I opened this a.m. I don't know what to do.*

I clicked the photo. It was a note, with a hand-scrawled game of Hangman. The stick figure was almost complete—missing just one leg—and underneath, it said, *Cancel fundraiser. One chance.*

I texted back, *Do you think this is from Monte?*

I don't know, she replied. *The studio was locked when I got here. No sign of another break-in.*

I typed, *File a police report so that it's documented if you need to build a case for harassment. We will come early tonight, and I want you to tell me everything that's happened, down to the last detail. We will get to the bottom of this.*

After hitting send, I looked at the picture again. The handwriting was stilted. Perhaps someone writing with their non-dominant hand.

Laurie gurgled, and I reached down to ruffle her hair.

"We can't let a bad man stop us from helping Mr. Jack and Miss Sharon, can we?" I asked her.

She grabbed my wrist and shoved my fingers into her mouth.

"No, we can't," I said with steely determination. I looked back at the poster on my screen. Jim had done a beautiful job with it. It boasted a classy silhouette of a swing dancing couple against a poodle-pink background. The white lettering looked like calligraphy. I skimmed the text, and my eyes stopped on the first line.

Pubic Dance

My hand flew to my mouth, and I rapidly replied to Jim. *PUBLIC dance, not PUBIC dance, omg!*

I hit *send* as fast as I could, lest he get tired of waiting and send that terrible typo to the printer. Then I composed a follow-up email.

Other than that, it is absolutely lovely. Make sure to get home on time—we need to go to the studio early. Love you!

A moment later, he replied, *LOL, good catch—this isn't THAT kind of dance establishment. See you soon!*

True to his word, he arrived home an hour before we needed to leave, and we ate a quick and simple dinner—sandwiches and Caesar salad from a bag—before getting dressed for the lesson. This time, I resolved to not be underdressed. I selected a maternity dress that felt like the 1950s—an empire-waisted black bodice with half sleeves, a red polka-dotted skirt, and a bow in the back.

It felt good to have something to dress up for, and I decided to put on my late grandmother's pearl earrings and add some red lipstick. The ensemble made me feel almost like a 1950s starlet. When I ignored the baby bump, I could even picture myself as a female version of some film noir private investigator.

"Samantha Spade," I said to the bathroom mirror in a gruff voice. "I didn't exactly believe your story, Mr. O'Shaughnessy—I believed your two hundred dollars."

"What's that?" called Jim from the bedroom.

"Nothing!" I scrunched my curls one last time, and came out of the bathroom to find Jim tying his tie. Laurie was sitting at his feet, happy as a clam with her stuffed ducky. "Hey, handsome."

Jim glanced up at me, and a smile curved his lips as he winked. I heard a loud banging, and I scooped up Laurie and scooted past Jim and out of the room.

"Mr. Kenny's here!" I sang to Laurie. But when I opened the door, there was no Kenny in sight. I frowned. *What was that noise?*

The banging sounded again. This time, it was clearly coming from the garage.

"Is Jo-Jo still here?" I called to Jim.

"His truck was here when I came in."

"A little late for him to still be working, isn't it?"

Jim came out of the room and shrugged. "I guess. But if it means he gets it done sooner, that's great."

He had a point, but still . . .

I opened the garage door and peeked inside. Jo-Jo was holding a wrench and stalking back and forth, muttering to himself, and . . .

What on earth was that smell?

Oh no!

An inch of water had pooled on the garage floor.

Jo-Jo caught sight of me and stopped his frantic pacing. He waved his arms and then gestured down to his galoshes. "No worries, lassie! Just a broken pipe. It'll all be taken care of! It'll be grand!"

He certainly liked that word.

I slammed the door shut and whirled to face Jim, wide-eyed. "I don't want to know," I squeaked.

Over Jim's shoulder, I spotted Kenny. "Oh, good, you're here!" I said, handing over Laurie. "Contractor's in the garage. Text me if you have any problems."

I practically bolted out the door, and Jim caught up to me at the car.

"What's wrong?" he asked.

"Something about a broken pipe," I muttered. "Why was he anywhere near a pipe? I'm calling Paula."

"A broken pipe?" Jim glanced back at the house.

Shaking my head, I opened the passenger door and climbed in. "Let's go. I have some investigating to do."

Paula didn't answer, so I left her a long, rambling message about the mess in the garage and the horrifying smell and Jo-Jo's reaction. I ended it by practically shrieking, "Call me back!"

When I hung up, Jim asked, "You sure we shouldn't go back and check on him?"

"And do what?"

He didn't reply. I'd made my point. Neither of us were handy enough to be of any help with whatever monstrous mayhem Jo-Jo had made in our garage.

We arrived at the studio, and I tried to push the garage situation out of my head. Jo-Jo would take care of it. It would be *grand.*

Petunia greeted us at the door. "Kate, I'm so glad you're here," she said. "I filed the police report, and they said there's nothing they can really do. They'll open a case, and I should let them know if anything else happens."

"Police report?" Jim asked.

We caught him up on the note, and I asked Petunia to tell me everything she remembered about the previous incidents.

There wasn't much. The items stolen in the break-in weren't of much monetary value, and there wasn't any other reason for someone to steal them—a lobby chair was taken, and so was a framed poster on the wall and a handful of children's costumes.

The dead bird—a pigeon—had been left a different day.

"What about the roof? Has it been fixed?" Jim asked.

"It's tarped to keep out moisture," she said. "We've got a roofer scheduled. It's in our costume closet, off one of the dance rooms."

"Can you show it to me?" I asked.

"Sure." She nodded. "This way."

While the three of us walked down the hall, I kept my eyes peeled for anything that stood out. "Do you have any security cameras?"

"We ordered one after the theft," she said. We turned in to a dance room and headed toward a door on the far side. "It was delayed in transit but should be here by the end of the week. The bird was weird, but we assumed it was just a freak thing. Bird flew in through an open door and happened to die on the dance floor. Bizarre, but there are a billion pigeons in San Francisco, right? But after the roof hole and the break-in . . . and now with this note . . ." Her voice caught, and we stopped in front of the door.

I rested a hand on her shoulder. "Get me a list of everyone who has keys to the studio. Do you know of anyone besides Monte who might have it in for the studio, or for Dave, Jack, or Eddie? Any angry former employees? Ex-clients who left on bad terms?"

She shook her head slowly. "I've tried and tried to think of who else might be behind this. There are so many possibilities, but none that make any sense to me. I'll get you a list of everyone who has a key, plus all of our former teachers. But we haven't had to fire anyone. And we haven't had any significant disputes with clients. There were a couple of minor things, but we figured the money wasn't worth a bad review and refunded them, so they left satisfied."

With that, she opened the door to the costume closet. Lace and glitter, organized by color, spilled off every shelf. Above, a hint of natural light peeked through a blue tarp. The hole was roughly cut, about four feet long and two feet wide.

"When did this happen?" I asked.

"That one we're not sure about," she said. "The closet doesn't get used most days. I went in to reorganize it on the first of the month—we sent a bunch of ballet students to a competition the week before, and they always throw costumes back in there every which way when they're done with them—and found the hole. It had to have been at least a few days earlier"—she pointed down at some rain damage on the floor—"but really could have been anytime in the previous three weeks. We had to have a bunch of the costumes professionally cleaned so they wouldn't mildew."

"What did the cops say about the hole?"

She chewed her lip. "That it was cut from the outside by someone who didn't really know what they were doing." Then she hesitated. "You know, going back to the question about who might have it in for the studio. There's always other professional dancers. The dance world can be cutthroat."

"So can the PI world."

We shared a smile, but then anguish overtook her face again. "I haven't told Dave about the note yet," she whispered. "He's been so stressed about everything. The studio isn't doing quite as well as he made out, and we don't know what any of us will do if it goes under. And Sharon and Jack have been through so much."

"Knock, knock," called an elegant voice. A tall blonde stood in the closet doorway. "Are you my next students?"

"Oh, I think Leo's our instructor," said Jim.

"Leo's off today," she said, extending a hand. "I'm Odette."

She was strikingly beautiful, perhaps twenty-four or twenty-five, with waist-length hair pulled back in a ponytail.

"Like the White Swan in *Swan Lake*?" I asked. That couldn't possibly be her real name, could it? It had to be a stage name, like Petunia.

Odette laughed, a genuine smile on her face. "My parents were both ballet dancers—and from Russia, so they took it all even more seriously—and I'm afraid they were sorely disappointed when I went into ballroom instead of ballet."

So it was her real name, apparently.

"Follow me," she said, "we're going to be two rooms down." She turned on her heel and practically glided toward the hallway. As I watched her go, I felt a little pang of jealousy and glanced down at my maternity dress. I'd felt so glamorous half an hour ago, but compared to Odette, I was drab and dowdy.

We waved to Petunia and walked after Odette, and Jim leaned in to whisper to me, "Maybe her parents just really wanted her to be rich."

I shot him an inquiring glance.

"Odette means *wealthy* in French, and . . . *little wealthy one,* I think, in Anglo-Saxon."

Furrowing my brows, I asked, "How on earth do you know that?"

"Went to elementary school with a stuck-up little wannabe socialite named Odette, and she made sure *everyone* knew."

I snorted as we strolled onto the dance floor.

"Let's review the steps you learned last time," Odette called from the far side of the room. "Rock step!"

"Here's to not tipping over," I muttered.

CHAPTER 5

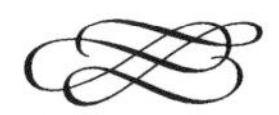

Odette's teaching style proved much gentler—or at least more patient—than Leo's. We made it through the triple step without incident, but when we tried to add the Charleston, I swiveled too hard while stepping back and found myself tipping over again.

Jim reached out to catch me, but I righted myself by flailing my arms. Cheeks burning, I glanced up at Miss Perfect White Swan, but she didn't seem disturbed.

"You're pregnant, right?" she asked. Then she hastened to add, "Not that I can tell by looking at you—Dave mentioned it."

"With twins," I said ruefully. "I mean, we're thrilled, of course. But finding bal—"

"Balance is always a learning curve in pregnancy, and with twins, it's double trouble. But you'll get the hang of it. You're a natural." She clapped her hands and turned to Jim. "Now, we're going to have some of our work cut out for us with you."

But the way she said it didn't raise my hackles like Leo had. She was matter-of-fact and direct, but easygoing and relaxed. I didn't get the sense that she was frustrated, and that made all the difference.

Jim gasped in mock affront, and I elbowed him in the ribs.

"Yeah," I said, "we've sure got our work cut out for us."

The rock step and triple step, which Jim had struggled with, were the easy ones. The Charleston required a lot more rhythm, which had never been Jim's specialty.

But rhythm could be taught. I hoped.

"If you guys are going to be part of the demonstration," Odette continued, "we need both of you to *look* like dancers."

"Excuse me, demonstration?" Jim's mouth fell open. "What do you mean?"

Odette tilted her head. "Oh, aren't you part of it? The demonstration at the fundraiser? I thought Dave and Petunia said . . ."

My forehead wrinkled. "Well, we did offer to help however they needed us. But Dave knows that Jim doesn't have a lot of dance experience."

Jim, his face two shades whiter than normal, stammered, "I-I'm just gonna go check on something."

He bolted for the door.

Just then, I heard a wailing baby in the lobby. My heart leaped. It sounded just like—

"Kenny?" Jim's voice.

My baby!

I took off running, my heart pounding. Why was Kenny here? Why was Laurie crying? Why—

I skidded to a stop in the lobby, and Laurie caught sight of me and lurched toward me, practically tearing herself from Kenny's arms. I pulled her close to me and kissed her forehead. Her cries didn't stop, but they quieted enough that we could speak over them.

"What's wrong?" I asked Kenny.

He grimaced and jumped up to sit on the front desk. "She pulled herself up on the coffee table and hit her head, and I couldn't get her to calm down. I tried calling."

Sure enough, there was a small lump on the top of Laurie's head. I internally berated myself for forgetting to turn my ringer on. I'd set it to vibrate earlier when Laurie was napping.

What kind of mother was I?

"Anyway," Kenny continued, "normally I'd just deal with the crying, but since she hit her head, I just wasn't sure what to do . . ."

"You did the right thing," I assured him. My heart thumped extra hard. I wasn't quite sure what to do, either. Her pupils looked fine. "Has she thrown up or anything?"

Kenny shook his head. "No, just cried and cried."

"I'll try to nurse her," I said. "Jim, can you try to get ahold of Dr. Clement?"

"Of course." Jim reached for his cell phone.

At that moment, I realized Odette had followed us out to the lobby. Kenny seemed to notice, too, because all signs of distress left his face. He stared at Odette, a deer-in-the-headlights expression making him look incredibly silly.

Laurie's cries softened to a gentle coo, and warmth suffused my chest. My baby had just needed her mama. I kissed her forehead again, careful to avoid the bump. "There's a sweet girl," I whispered.

For privacy, I withdrew back to the room we'd been dancing in—I remembered a chair in the corner where I could sit in relative solitude. As I stepped away, I heard Kenny's voice—half an octave lower than normal—say, "Hey. I'm Ken."

Ken? I snorted. Odette was gorgeous, of course, and Kenny was between girlfriends, so I wasn't surprised he'd fallen head over heels at the sight of her. But unfortunately for Kenny, there was no way elegant, worldly Odette was going to be impressed by a starstruck eighteen-year-old.

Poor Kenny.

By the time Laurie finally calmed, Jim had talked to the nurse at Dr. Clement's office and gotten a list of warning signs to watch for.

"Should we just go home?" I asked. "I'm not really in the mood for the last twenty minutes of the lesson."

"Me neither," grumbled Jim, glancing at our reflections in the room's floor-to-ceiling mirrors. "But we've gotta schedule a lot more lessons if we're going to be part of the dance demonstration."

I stood and shifted Laurie to my hip. "You can say no if you're not comfortable with it."

Jim looked aghast. "What? No. I-I just panicked. That's all. We promised we'd help out however they needed us. It will be fine."

We reached the hallway, and Laurie entwined her fingers in my hair. When we walked into the lobby, I stopped short. Kenny was leaning up against the wall, and Odette was laughing at something he'd said.

Wait, really?

I looked at Kenny. I supposed he looked a tad older than eighteen. Odette must not realize she was talking to someone who was barely out of high school.

"Should we head back?" I asked Kenny. "The cash to pay you is at the house. We can order you some wings as hazard pay."

He didn't even glance away from Odette's face. "Nah, I'll stay here a little longer. I drove the van. We can square up later."

"Okay," I said slowly, "I'm going to need the car seat out of your van."

That seemed to wake him up, at least. We got the car seat, and Jim and I headed home with Laurie.

"Lovestruck puppy," I murmured as I closed my car door. "He can only get burned falling for a woman like that."

"I don't know." Jim backed out of the parking lot. "I fell in love with a woman like that and somehow got her to marry me."

I tried to scowl, but that man sure had a way of putting a smile on my face. "She's older and won't take him seriously," I protested. Then I remembered. "Oh! We're supposed to meet with Dave and Petunia tomorrow afternoon to go over some of the fundraiser plans, and I forgot to ask Kenny to babysit!"

"Just text him," said Jim. "He won't hear a word you're saying if we drive back and ask him in person. He's too twitterpated."

"You're not wrong," I muttered, and fired off a text to Kenny.

We pulled into the driveway, and I was relieved to see that Jo-Jo's truck was gone and the house was dark—no light peeking out through the garage door seam. He'd finally gone home.

I unbuckled a sleeping Laurie from her car seat, and we headed toward the door. She whimpered, and then curled into me and fell into a deeper sleep. A soft smile lit my face. It would be hard when I had a one-year-old and twin babies, but oh, how I loved being a mom. Jim unlocked the door, and we stepped inside.

And then the smell hit me.

"What on earth?" Jim exclaimed.

I made a guttural noise and staggered back. *What is that smell?* It was putrid, like the world's worst poopy diaper had rotted and given birth to a whole army of rotten poopy diapers. Like a zombie apocalypse of poopy diapers.

The garage flood!

I ran into the kitchen. Jo-Jo had left a note on the counter.

Pipe busted was of sewer variety. Stayed late to fix, so not leaking anymore. Suggest opening windows and DO NOT OPEN DOOR TO GARAGE.

Nausea overcame me, and I bolted back outside and dry-heaved into the bushes while keeping a firm grip on Laurie.

A moment later, Jim joined me, his complexion a shade of green I'd never seen before.

"How much you want to bet that Laurie's head bump was just the final straw and Kenny was fleeing that smell?" Jim asked.

"He could have at least given us a warning!" I looked hopelessly at the house. "What will we do? We can't . . . sleep in that!"

"I opened the windows," said Jim. "Let's get a hotel tonight."

"And leave the windows open? What if someone breaks in?"

Jim laughed aloud. "Think they're gonna stick around in that smell to steal anything? There are plenty of available burglary jobs in the city that don't require a trip to Sewer Sauna."

He was right. We couldn't stay overnight. "My mom will put us up," I said. "It'll be crowded, but we can bring Whiskers. I don't want her stuck in that stench either."

* * *

"KENNY STILL HASN'T TEXTED ME BACK," I SAID THE NEXT MORNING AS I sat at my mom's table and stared morosely at my phone. "He always texts me back."

A tendril of concern coiled in the back of my mind. Odd things *had* been happening at the studio recently. Should I be worried about Kenny? Whiskers jumped up in my lap and started kneading my jeans.

"Well, I'll watch Laurie." Mom set a cup of steaming coffee in front of me. "Decaf for you, my dear. I have to keep some around for Galigani, you know. You and Jim go to your meeting, and I'll get in my grandma snuggles. Maybe we'll even go shopping and pick out a few things for the twins."

Dreadful visions filled my mind—two screaming squirrel buses to match the yodeling chipmunk bus. Or bags full of yarn in cacophonous, mismatched colors so my mom could knit the babies tiny caterpillar suits. Or . . .

But Mom was an excellent grandma, and I needed a babysitter. Though part of me wanted to just bring Laurie along to the meeting, I really needed to give Dave and Petunia my full attention. It was important to get this fundraiser right. "Thank you," I said. "But really, you don't need to go shopping. Just a quiet day—"

Mom waved off my objections, and I didn't try to argue. If she was going to be free babysitting, they could do what she wanted for the day.

Besides, there would be no dissuading her.

Jim strolled out of the bathroom, his hair still damp from his shower. "Laurie still sleeping?" he asked, kissing me on the forehead and glancing toward the portable crib that Mom kept around.

"She went back to sleep after she nursed this morning," I said, scratching Whiskers on the chin. "Looks like her head bonk is going to be just fine. Mom's going to babysit while we meet with Dave and Petunia."

Laurie started fussing, and Mom jumped to her feet and pulled her out of the portable crib before I could react. "I'll watch her now," she said. "You guys still need to prep for the meeting, right?"

Several hours later, we walked into the studio for our two o'clock meeting. Jim carried a folio holding three different sample flyers—I'd made sure that each and every one of them spelled *public* correctly—and I had a legal pad and three color-coded pens.

"Back here!" called Dave.

We walked down the hall, past several dance rooms, and found the office at the back of the building. Piles of paper rose like skyscrapers from the desk, and Dave and Petunia were staring at a laptop screen. Petunia's face could only be described as *frazzled*. But when we stepped through the doorframe, she managed a tired wave.

"Thanks so much for coming!" Dave exclaimed. "I think we've hit a wall on what we can do without a fresh pair of eyes."

"Let's dig in!" said Jim. "Dave, can we finalize the marketing posters while Kate and Petunia talk logistics—ticket sales, radio promotions, dance floor layout?"

Dave and Jim conferred near the computer, and Petunia and I pulled up chairs to the other end of the desk. Petunia drummed her fingers on the desk and gestured to my notepad. "Do we want to get layout down first? That way we know how many people we can accommodate, which will help us figure out how many tickets to sell?"

I uncapped a green pen and nodded at her. "How many square feet of space do we have?"

"So, our dance rooms are separated by dividers, not solid walls, so we'll take those out to make a giant dance floor. That will give us—"

A feminine shriek sounded from somewhere in the building, and I whirled toward the sound. Then I heard the scuffling of running feet, and two figures appeared in the doorway. Odette, her blonde ponytail flying out behind her, and . . .

"Kenny?" I demanded.

Kenny's eyes were wide, and Odette was blubbering like she might be about to burst into hysterics. She lurched for the small office trash can and vomited into it.

"Come quick," said Kenny in a strained voice. "Someone's been murdered."

CHAPTER 6

"Murdered?" squeaked Petunia.

But I was already shoving past Kenny and Odette. "No one touch anything!" I yelled. "Dave, call 911. Jim, call Galigani. Kenny, show me the body."

That strange Hangman note. The memory whirled in my head. It hadn't just been harassment. It had been a warning.

A deadly serious warning.

I started off at a run and then slowed down to a dignified jog to avoid jostling the babies too much.

Kenny caught up to me. "This way."

I followed him into the second dance room on the hall. The light was on, and on the far side, the costume closet door was open, and a pair of feet were sticking out.

Taking a breath to steel myself, I strode toward the body. It was a man, wearing a suit, lying on his stomach.

With a knife sticking out of his back.

Well, I guess that's why they concluded it was murder.

My heart sank at the familiar head of gray hair. "Oh, no. Leo," I whispered.

The grumpy British dance teacher had danced his last tango.

I took a deep breath and walked in a slow circle around the body, careful to not touch anything. "Tell me everything," I said to Kenny. "You said you found him."

Kenny audibly gulped. "Yeah. Odette and I'd been working on a music video all day."

I raised an eyebrow at him, and he protested, "I'm doing a jazzy tuba cover of 'Billie Jean,' and I thought it'd be classy to film clips of some real ballroom dancing."

"Do you know how to dance ballroom?" I squatted next to poor Leo and visually inspected the knife wound. Something didn't look quite right about it—maybe it was just the dark suit jacket, but it seemed like there wasn't enough blood for the knife to have been the killing blow. Galigani would know if I was onto something or not.

"'Course!" said Kenny, puffing out his chest when I glanced his direction. Then he glanced down at the body and grimaced. "I mean, not as well as Odette or anything. But I'm a musician. I got rhythm. I held my own."

"Okay, right. Sorry. So, you were out with Odette, and then you came here for . . ."

"Costuming," said Kenny. "We'd worked out most of the choreography, and Odette said we could borrow some costumes from the studio."

I glanced back toward the open closet door and the shelves brimming with colorful, sparkly fabrics.

The costume closet. We'd just been here the day before looking at the hole in the roof.

Careful to not tip forward, I stood and strode into the closet, then looked up. The tarp had been torn away, and a big rope net dangled from the ceiling.

Interesting. That was new. I snapped a few pictures on my cell phone.

"Kate!" Galigani called from behind me.

I turned around and waved at him. "Oh, I'm so glad you got here before the homicide detectives did. Tell me what you see."

His lips were set in a grim line as he looked at the body. "Someone stabbed him in the back when he was already dead to make us think he was killed by a knife."

I pumped my fist, then realized we had an audience, and regained a sober, respectful expression. Petunia and Dave, Jim and Eddie, Odette, and two dance teachers I didn't recognize stood in the doorway. Odette's face was a peculiar shade of green, and Jim placed a comforting arm on her shoulder.

"I thought that might be the case," I said quietly. "About the wound. It didn't look right to me."

Galigani shot me an approving look. "You're learning."

Dave took a tentative step toward us. "Is that . . ."

"It's Leo," I called. "I'm so sorry."

For his part, Dave looked every bit as nauseated as Odette. "Was he . . ."

"It looks like murder," said Galigani. "And a murder someone went through the trouble to stage afterward, so it would draw attention to itself. Do you have any enemies? Someone who would want to see your business taken down?"

Sirens wailed outside, and a few moments later, a couple of cops and Nick Dowling, the medical examiner, came into the room. I made a face at Sergeant McNearny's appearance—he and I had butted heads from the beginning—but I was relieved to see my friend Deb Fisher with him.

Deb shot me a broad smile. "Heard it was Jim who called it in, and figured you'd be here somehow, so I hitchhiked with Sergeant McGrumpy."

"I heard that," grumbled McNearny.

"I rest my case," said Deb with a grin.

"Galigani, what do we know?" McNearny squatted by the body.

"You'll have to ask Kate. She was here when they found him."

McNearny sighed dramatically. "Of course she was. She's like a vulture with a sixth sense for where a dead body's gonna fall out of the sky."

"I think this one might have really fallen out of the sky," I retorted. "Get a look at this hole in the roof. Kenny here and Odette, the blonde over there, found him."

Two more cops came in, and Deb waved at them. "Yo, let's secure the crime scene!"

McNearny pulled Kenny aside to take his statement. Kenny repeated what he'd told me about the music video, and then added, "When we opened the door to the costume closet, the body fell to the ground right in front of us."

"That might mean the killer dumped the body just at the wrong time, when someone happened to be opening the closet," Galigani said. "Which could give us a good place to start for an alibi."

"Or it could mean the killer rigged the body to fall as soon as the closet door was opened," Deb said, shining a flashlight on something inside. "And I think it's the latter. Look at this." I followed her in, and she pointed to a hook on the backside of the door and the rope netting I'd noticed earlier.

"The net is connected to the back of the door on one side!" I exclaimed.

"And to the ceiling on the other side. As soon as the door was pushed inward, *bam*! Falling body."

I walked back onto the dance floor. The other cops had cordoned off the area with caution tape and were now taking statements from Odette and Petunia.

Dave was sitting along the back wall, his shoulders slumped.

"Dave!" I called, striding toward him. "How often is the costume closet used?"

"A lot when our students are headed off to competitions or leading up to our recitals, but we didn't have anything on the schedule for the next couple of weeks. No reason we'd have opened it until we were assigning costumes for the fundraiser."

"Is it usually locked?" I stopped when I reached him.

"No. We don't keep it locked. Kate." His voice took on an intensity I'd never heard from him before. "Will you solve this for us? Will you take the case? I can't pay a lot right now, but if we do a payment plan . . ."

"I'd be happy to take the case," I said. "And don't worry about the money. We'll work something out. Maybe if the fundraiser makes more than enough money to cover Sharon's fertility treatments, you can pay me half of whatever is left."

"No, that might not be any money at all. I can't ask—"

"I insist." I locked eyes with him. "This is important."

Out of the corner of my eye, I saw Odette flee the room, her shoulders heaving.

The officer she'd been talking to gestured to Dave. "Just finished up with her. Can you give your statement now?"

Glancing around and not seeing anything else that demanded my attention, I followed Odette into the hall. She wasn't out there, but on a hunch, I headed to the women's restroom.

Sure enough, she was there, leaning over the sink, pale and trembling.

"You okay?" I asked.

She glanced up at me and managed a weak laugh. "I think there's nothing left in my stomach to throw up, but I just can't seem to stop gagging."

"Were you and Leo close?"

She hesitated, and then turned the faucet on and splashed water on her face. "Not really. He was kind of obnoxious, actually. Ugh, that sounds awful now that he's dead." She shut off the water and pulled a paper towel out of the dispenser. "But, you just don't expect to have a dead body fall right in front of you when you're opening a closet you've opened a hundred times before. And then for it to be someone you know . . ." She closed her eyes. "I'm sorry. I'll get a handle on myself. You see this stuff all the time. You must think I'm being ridiculous."

"You're not being ridiculous." I leaned back against the wall. "It's a shock the first time you find a dead body. The second time too. And it's a lot worse when it's someone you've known a long time. I've been there."

"Ken said he's helped you out with some cases," she said. "Is that true, or just a line he feeds to girls?"

My nose wrinkled at the name *Ken,* but I just responded, "Oh, Kenny's been invaluable. Even saved my life a couple times. Pretty good for a high schooler."

She visibly jolted. "High schooler?"

Ah, there we go. My work here was done.

"Oh." She blinked. "I . . . thought he was older. He said he was in college.

"Well, he's taking community college classes now," I said. "He just turned eighteen recently."

Apologies to Kenny, but there were millions of pretty girls in his age bracket. I'd helped set him up with a few. No good could come of an eighteen-year-old boy getting entangled with a twenty-five-year-old pro dancer.

No good at all.

"I better go. Sorry," she said, pushing past me and out the door.

I glanced in the mirror, brushed away a stray fleck of eyeliner, and returned to the crime scene. The medical examiner was just zipping up the body bag.

Galigani beckoned me over. "Looks like some defensive bruises on Leo's feet," he said. "We'll know more when the autopsy comes back tomorrow."

Deb joined us. "We've gotten statements from pretty much everyone," she said in a low voice. "I don't much like the two ballet teachers, Kim and Todd. You met them yet?"

I shook my head and glanced around the room, but besides the cops, the only people still here were Jim and Dave.

Deb continued, "They may be able to alibi out—depends on what the ME concludes about time of death—but they had nothing but good things to say about Leo, and everyone else says the two of them hated Leo's guts."

"The good news," said Galigani, "is that Petunia said she went into the costume closet when she opened the studio this morning at nine. Something about checking on some sort of skirt and matching tie combo, to see how many they had for the upcoming dance."

"And Leo didn't fall out of the sky then," I said. "So regardless of when he died, we know someone put him there in the closet between about nine and two."

"Exactly!" Deb high-fived me.

"Anything else we can learn here?" I asked Galigani.

"Let's call it a day," he replied. "We'll make a plan this evening and start chasing down leads first thing tomorrow. And . . . one more thing, kid." He gave Deb a long, steely look, and she raised her hands in surrender and retreated.

"Girl's night with Paula soon?" she called as she walked away.

"You got it!" I turned back to Galigani and lifted an eyebrow. "What's the secret from Deb?"

Galigani pulled at his collar. "You gonna have a free couple hours sometime soon? Next weekend maybe?"

"We'll see how the case treats us," I said slowly. "What is it?"

"Was wondering if you might help me with some shopping."

I stared at him. "Shopping?"

"Maybe at a jewelry store. You could tell me what your mom likes. You know. For rings."

My heart pounded in my ears. "Rings?"

Galigani looked hurt. "I mean, I know your mom and I haven't been a couple for all that long, but when you're our age—"

"Oh! I didn't mean it like that!" I exclaimed. "I'm thrilled. You just took me by surprise."

His face morphed into an expression of relief, and guilt tugged at my chest. Should I warn him that Mom might not feel ready to commit?

Nope, I decided. Surely Mom wouldn't start running around with Hank if she knew how serious Galigani was about her.

Surely.

To Do:

1. Research best baby-proofing system.
2. ~~Land new client? (Maybe Dave's studio?)~~ Solve Leo's murder.
3. Help Galigani shop for engagement rings.
4. Chase off Hank.

CHAPTER 7

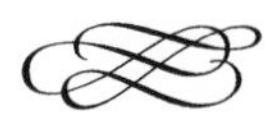

By the time Jim and I arrived home with Laurie and Whiskers, the stench of zombie diapers had mostly dissipated. I sighed in relief.

"What a week!" I said as I opened Whiskers' carrier. She scrambled under the couch and vanished.

Jim sank onto the couch with Laurie in his arms. "I feel so bad for Dave and his brothers. The hits just keep on coming. Do you think Monte did it?"

"That makes the most sense," I said, sitting beside him. "I'll certainly be interested to hear if he has an alibi. Deb thought the ballet teachers were suspicious too."

Laurie reached for me, and I pulled her out of Jim's lap and cuddled her close.

Jim ran a hand through his hair. "Doesn't seem like—"

My phone rang. I glanced at the caller ID. *Kenny.* I held up a finger to signal Jim to wait a moment, and answered, "Hey, what's up?"

"Hey, I just saw you guys pull in," Kenny said. "Mind if I come over? I just . . . everything that happened and . . ."

"You need to talk about it?" I asked gently.

"Yeah."

"Come on over," I said in a warm voice. "We'll break out the ice cream."

Not ten seconds later, a knock sounded on the door. I chuckled. "He didn't even wait for us to pick up before he started walking over."

I ushered Kenny inside, and he wrinkled his nose.

"Still doesn't smell great in here, does it?" he asked.

"A lot better than it did," Jim answered wryly.

Kenny laughed, but it seemed strained. "You have a point. What was up with that smell, anyway?"

Jim briefly explained the human tornado that was Jo-Jo, and the burst sewer pipe. Though Kenny seemed engaged, I could tell he was having a hard time. His enthusiasm seemed dimmed.

Poor kid. He'd gotten into his fair share of scrapes helping me out, but it was still traumatic to find a dead body like that. He was still so young.

"How are you doing?" I asked.

He hesitated, then shifted in his seat. "It was a hard day. Well, not the first part. The first part was great. Odette is . . ." His eyes took on a dreamy look, and I felt a little trace of guilt that I'd interfered. He cleared his throat and continued, "When we found the dead guy, it—"

His phone rang. He glanced at it, and his eyes brightened. "That's Odette."

He answered the phone, and I looked helplessly at Jim. Odette was calling Kenny? Even after I'd told her he was eighteen?

"Yeah," said Kenny into the phone. "I can explain. Definitely. Now?" He shot to his feet and headed toward the door, waving at us. "Sorry, guys," he called. "Can we finish this later? I need to go see her."

He was outside before either of us had a chance to respond.

I gave a long sigh. "I tried. I really did."

Jim gave me a wry look. "You're not his mom, you know."

"But I'm kind of like his fun aunt." I stuck my tongue out. "The permissive one who doesn't interfere unless the kid is about to do something really, really stupid."

Jim shook his head. "Well, be careful how you interfere. It might make him want to date the girl even more."

* * *

SORRY, NO CAN DO, READ KENNY'S TEXT MESSAGE. *SPENDING DAY WITH odette. she doesn't want to be alone.*

I grunted and glanced at the clock. I was supposed to meet Galigani at the precinct in an hour to look at the autopsy report, and I needed a babysitter. If Kenny was off making eyes at Odette, I'd have to go to my backup list.

First, I called Mom.

"Oh, I'm so sorry, darling," she said before I was halfway through my question. "I'm shopping for some ingredients to test some 1950s-style recipes for the fundraiser. I found this really interesting one for ham and bananas hollandaise."

"I'm sorry, what?"

"Ham and bananas hollandaise. It's bananas, wrapped in slices of ham, and slathered in hollandaise sauce."

Even for Mom, that sounded insane. "Do you . . . think maybe we should stick to dishes that might be a little more popular?"

"But this is authentic! I found it in your grandmother's old cookbook. I'm also getting stuff to try out a savory popsicle."

"A savory . . . popsicle?"

"This recipe uses pork, beans, and ketchup." Sometimes I couldn't tell if the glee in her voice was genuine, or if she knew I thought she was being crazy.

Probably both—and probably she was determined to prove me wrong by making savory popsicles a huge hit.

"Um . . ." I pinched the bridge of my nose and sighed. Laurie had just pulled herself to a standing position next to the coffee table and was chewing on the corner of my legal pad. Swooping her up, I said, "You know, that sounds great. See how they taste, and we'll go from there. I'm sure Paula can watch Laurie."

I dialed Paula next. No answer. I dialed again. Still no answer.

She did text me back, though. *Sorry. Can't. With a potential client. Will call back this afternoon.*

I groaned and buried my head in my hands. Jim had meetings all day, so he couldn't play stay-at-home dad. Dropping a kiss on top of

Laurie's head, I murmured, "Guess we're a dynamic duo today, little duck. Do you want to go see the nice officers at the station?"

I went to dress Laurie in her little blue dress that looked sort of like a policewoman uniform, but it was a little too tight. "Mama's sweet girl is growing so fast, huh?" I cooed.

In the end, we settled on a no-nonsense pair of pink leggings and a little white dress with a gray sweater.

I wheeled Laurie into the precinct, and she gave a big grin to the cop sitting at the front desk. The officer waved back, and Galigani came in behind us.

"Hey, Travis," Galigani said to the desk officer. "We're here to talk to Nick."

The officer waved us back, and on a whim, I said, "Let me run by Deb's office first."

I knocked on the doorframe and stuck my head in. "Hey, Deb. You doing anything?"

She glanced up from a thick pile of paperwork. "Nothing interesting. You got something better for me?"

I pointed down at the stroller. "Galigani and I are headed down to meet with the ME, and I don't really want to give Laurie her first introduction to a dead body until she's at least *nine* months old."

Deb snorted and pushed back from her desk. "Leave her here. We'll get along just fine until you're back."

"Thank you!" I exclaimed, wheeling Laurie all the way inside. "I owe you one!"

"I've been staring at paperwork all day," she said with an eyeroll. "At this point, my eyes are glazing over and I'd much rather be playing with this cutie."

"Anything else I should know about the case?"

"Nothing significant. That Monte guy is pretty suspicious, but you knew that already."

"That's the first lead I'm gonna run down after I leave," I called as I headed out the door.

Galigani and I went down to the basement, where the Nick the medical examiner was sitting in front of a computer screen.

"Whatcha got?" Galigani asked.

Nick hit *print* and spun his chair to face us. "I'll give you a copy of the autopsy report," he said in his husky voice, "but the short version is that we're looking at a poisoning."

"So, we were right," said Galigani. "Leo was already dead when he was knifed in the back."

"What would the killer gain by making it so obvious that it's a murder?" I asked.

"Could be trying to frame someone," offered Galigani.

The printer finished spitting out the report, and Nick handed it to Galigani.

"The poison was vercuronium bromide, a paralyzing agent that's pretty commonly used in small doses by anesthesiologists. But the intent here was clearly murder. He had several times the lethal limit in his system," said Nick. "It stopped his heart."

Galigani glanced through the report, and my gaze landed on a small shelf of superhero figurines above Nick's desk. I hadn't taken him for a comics nerd.

"You collect those?" I asked, gesturing to the shelf.

He grinned, and I suddenly could picture exactly what he must have looked like as a chubby-cheeked five-year-old. "Just a little. Marvel only. No DC."

"So," I said, squinting and trying to sort out which was which, hoping I wasn't getting it backward. "Yes, to Captain Marvel and no, to Wonder Woman?"

"Well," he said, gesturing to a photo on the desk, "my wife tells me I have to make an exception for Wonder Woman."

The picture showed Nick and a pretty redhead, dressed up as superheroes. The woman—his wife, I presumed—was wearing a Wonder Woman costume. I didn't recognize Nick's costume, but it looked vaguely familiar.

"Halloween?" I asked.

"Comic con." His smile told me he knew it was impossibly nerdy but didn't care.

Galigani cleared his throat. "So, bottom line is that our vic was poisoned with a paralyzing agent but had time to fight back before it killed him. And he was stabbed postmortem."

"Which means the killer may have had the knife to threaten him," I said slowly. "We need to figure out if Leo was the target, or if this is about a vendetta against the studio."

"Or both." Galigani rolled up the sheaf of papers. "Two birds with one stone, maybe?"

We thanked Nick and left, picking up Laurie on our way out of the precinct. Galigani walked us to our car. I took a deep breath, enjoying the warm sunshine and fresh breeze.

"Listen kid," Galigani said, leaning up against the passenger door. "About that shopping trip for your mom, I—"

"Yo, Kate!" Deb yelled, bursting into the parking lot and running toward us.

"Yeah?" I called.

She was out of breath by the time she reached us. "You weren't in the room when we found that note, were you? And Galigani, you were talking to that guy who owns the studio. Did you see it? Did McGrumpy tell you about it?"

I shook my head and glanced at Galigani. He appeared to be as in-the-dark as I was.

"What note?" he and I asked in unison.

Deb pumped a fist triumphantly. "The dude was holding a note. The dead guy."

Another note? "What did it say?"

She pulled out her phone and winked at me. "Don't tell anyone I snapped a shot of evidence, okay? I'm doing you a favor."

"My lips are sealed."

Galigani grunted his assent, though I suspected that, as an ex-cop, he was probably cringing.

Deb pulled up the picture on her phone, and my heart pounded faster. It was another Hangman drawing. This time, the message said, *Game over. Try again. Cancel the fundraiser, or someone dies on the dance floor.*

CHAPTER 8

"I need to make a fresh to-do list," I groaned, glancing at my ratty notecard and shifting Laurie to my other hip.

Paula, wearing a pink pencil skirt and ruffled blouse, peered over my shoulder, then gazed again at the huge mirrored wall on the dance floor at the studio. "What if we drape some gauzy fabric over this whole thing?" she said. "You know, the stuff with the twinkle lights? It'd be an easy way to hide the giant mirror."

Petunia and Dave had pulled out all the dividers so Paula and I could see the whole floor as one unit.

"Oh!" Paula snapped her fingers and pointed at my notecard. "Don't bother researching baby-proofing systems. We tried out like five different ones when Danny started getting into everything. He was a regular Houdini. I can't remember the name of the brand that worked, but I'll take a picture of the logo when I get home and send it to you."

With a triumphant cry, I crossed "Research best baby-proofing system" off my list.

"There we go!" I cooed to Laurie. "We're getting ahead of the game before you start pulling things out of cupboards!"

Laurie just squirmed.

"Now to figure out how to throw the best fundraiser of all time and catch a killer before someone else ends up dead," I muttered.

"No big deal," quipped Paula. "A day in the life." She scowled at the mirrored wall and tapped her fingers together. "The gauzy fabric and twinkle lights would be pretty, but they're not particularly 1950s-themed. I think we can come up with something better."

"Daaarling!" cried my mother's voice. I spun around to find Mom striding across the dance floor, her wedge heels clacking on the wood. Galigani followed in her wake, carrying a platter.

"Oh!" Paula called. "You come bearing food. Are you trying to sabotage my diet?"

I eyed Paula's slim figure. "You've already lost your baby weight," I grumbled.

"Well, I'm not having anymore," she snickered back at me.

"Grapefruit baked Alaska!" declared Mom, pulling Laurie from my arms. "Come out to the lobby—we'll set up on the front desk and sample it."

"No savory popsicles, then?" I asked in relief.

She quirked her lips. "Those almost made the cut, but I thought it might be better to focus on sweets."

Translation: They'd tasted terrible.

As we headed to the lobby, Paula took the lead, chattering with Mom. Galigani and I fell in step behind them.

"So, kid, where are we at on the case?" he asked.

"I talked to Petunia, Odette, Kenny, and all three brothers," I replied. "And I have an interview set up with those ballet teachers tomorrow. They kept putting me off. Can't seem to get in touch with Monte, but Deb said the police were bringing him in for an interview, so maybe she can sneak us a copy of the transcript. Did you look up the ballet teachers in the database? Anything on their record?"

"Clean criminal records," he said, "although, I did a little more digging. You know I'm pretty thorough."

I smiled. Nothing like Galigani poking around for a compliment.

"You are. That's why we're the best."

He snorted. "I'm going to ignore that *we* for the moment—"

"I just meant you're a good teacher. I'm learning from the best and—"

He waved a hand around, already tired of the subject. "So, what I found is that Todd was a suspect in the poisoning of a fellow dancer back when he was in high school. The girl survived but was too traumatized to dance again."

My hand flew to my mouth. "What was the motive for the poisoning?"

"They thought he did it for his girlfriend, who was also a dancer and who was auditioning for the same leading role as the victim."

"Like poor Nancy Kerrigan!" I said.

"Only not the knee and not figure-skating, but whatever." Galigani grunted.

I elbowed him. "You knew what I meant."

He nodded and finally broke into a smile.

"Was Kim the girlfriend, by any chance?" I asked.

"No," Galigani said. "Another dancer. He seems to have met Kim about five years ago. They were the leads in *Romeo and Juliet*."

We came into the lobby to find Dave and Petunia already there. Mom—while somehow still perfectly balancing Laurie—opened a bag of paper plates and cut into the baked Alaska with a plastic knife. With a suspicious expression, I accepted a small slice topped with a maraschino cherry. I took a bite, preparing myself for something totally inedible. Instead, tangy sweetness exploded in my mouth. It was . . . surprisingly good.

"Not bad, Mom," I said. "What's in it?"

"Grapefruit with a brown meringue, topped with a maraschino cherry." She loaded her own slice onto a plate. "I had to buy a whole truckload of maraschino cherries, I'll have you know—so many 1950s recipes use them."

I popped the cherry in my mouth. "Were there maraschino cherries in the savory popsicles?"

"As a matter of fact—"

I shuddered and tuned her out.

"This is great, Vera!" said Petunia, finishing off her piece. "I'd love it if you made this for the fundraiser!" She stepped forward to cut another slice and visibly winced.

"What's wrong?" I asked.

She reached down and rubbed her knee. "Just a sore joint," she said. "Thankfully one of our students is a pharmacist, and he should be bringing by my anti-inflammatory gel any minute—"

Warning bells rang in my head just as Hank walked in the door. *Oh no.*

Hank and Galigani locked eyes and stared at each other, hostility shadowing their faces. Hank recovered first.

"Vera! Galigani! So good to see you both!" He held a plastic bag out toward Petunia. "Got the gel for you, Miss Petal."

"You're an angel!" cried Petunia as she accepted the bag. "You really didn't have to come all this way."

He scoffed. "It's not far at all, and I didn't mind *swinging by* on my lunch break."

Mom giggled at the pun. Right in front of Galigani! If I'd been any closer, I'd have elbowed her in the ribs.

"Hank," she said, "you must try this grapefruit baked Alaska I'm testing out for the fundraiser. Tell me what you think—and be honest."

"I'm always honest," he said with a wink. He took a slice and closed his eyes as he savored the first bite. "I think you missed your calling as a chef, Vera. You should open a restaurant!"

I stepped forward, but before I could say anything, Hank reached out and tickled Laurie's foot. Laurie giggled, and Galigani and I glanced at each other and rolled our eyes.

The door opened again, and two tall, beautiful people came in—a man and a woman. I vaguely recognized them—I was pretty sure they were here the day we found Leo's body. Were they Kim and Todd?

Petunia waved. "Hey, guys! Want to try out a dessert?"

The new arrivals looked at the baked Alaska as if it might bite them.

"No, thank you," said the woman in a smooth voice. "I have to watch what I eat. Ballet is tough that way."

I eyed her figure. She was impossibly slim. Oh, one bite of dessert would kill her? She should try being pregnant with twins. I vengefully forked another bite of baked Alaska into my mouth.

They passed by us without another word, and Petunia shook her head when they disappeared from view down the hall.

"That's Kim and Todd," she said to me in a low voice. "They think they're better than all the other dancers because they teach ballet. They get on my nerves, to tell you the truth."

"Oh, I have an interview with them tomorrow about the case. What should I know about them?"

Petunia looked like she'd tasted something sour. "Besides that they're stuck-up and want to make everyone around them miserable?"

I snorted. "Why don't you tell me how you really feel?"

Petunia took another bite of baked Alaska. When she swallowed, she said, "They've been working here for three years. They definitely have an attitude, but they bring in ballet students, and that's good money. They help keep us afloat, so we put up with them. They didn't like Leo, but, then again, they don't really like anyone here."

"What were they doing before?" I asked.

"This is their first teaching gig. They were professional dancers until this. Went to good ballet schools, headlined for some major dance companies. Might have been able to make more money teaching in New York, but Todd's mom is here in San Francisco, and she's got some health challenges."

"Did they have anything against Leo?"

Petunia quirked her lips. "Like I said, they didn't like him or anyone else. I really don't know that there was any grudge big enough for . . . that, though."

"Excuse me, Kate," Hank said, interrupting our conversation. "Are you going to be here for a while longer?"

"About another hour, I think," I answered.

He excused himself, and I watched him leave with open curiosity. Galigani seemed to relax the moment Hank left the studio.

Laurie started fussing, and I took her from Mom. That seemed to soothe her for a moment, but then she started squirming and fussing again. I looked down at her. "You can't possibly be hungry yet, little duck. You ate a half hour ago."

Her cries got a little louder, and she reached for Galigani. I glanced from Laurie to Galigani and back again. Galigani's eyes lit up as he pulled her into his arms. She immediately settled down.

"Well, then," he said with a note of pride in his voice.

"You look very grandfatherly right now," I said, hoping Mom was paying attention.

"I feel very grandfatherly right now," he replied. Laurie cuddled into the crook of his neck.

"Oh, how perfect," said Mom. "We can get some planning done while you and Laurie keep each other company!"

"I'd be delighted," said Galigani with a little bow.

It was a funny picture—gruff detective Albert Galigani reduced to a puddle of mush by a little baby. But it felt right.

Hank was nice enough, but he needed to go—there was no question.

Paula, Mom, and I went back down to the dance floor—which was a little smaller now that Kim and Todd had put the furthest set of dividers back to give themselves a room for the class they were about to teach—and by the time the hour was up, we had the whole menu planned, along with the layout of the room and most of the decor.

We were putting the final touches on the plans for the lighting when Hank walked in carrying a beautiful wooden rocking horse.

Galigani, who was reading a board book with Laurie in the corner of the room, shot a vengeful look at Hank's back.

"I brought this for Laurie!" said Hank. "She's just the right age to enjoy a rocking horse, isn't she?"

My mom's hand flew to her chest. "You shouldn't have!" she cried.

The rocking horse was intricately carved out of dark wood. I couldn't even begin to imagine how expensive it had been.

"I absolutely should have," Hank said, turning toward Galigani and Laurie. "Bring her over here, see if she likes it."

From the look on Galigani's face, there was nothing he wanted to do less. But politeness won out, and he swung Laurie up and brought her over. Hank set the rocking horse down, and Galigani set her next to it.

I found my voice. "Hank, this is so generous of you, but it's too much—"

"I insist," said Hank. We locked eyes, and a look of deep sincerity shone through his gaze. "It's a free gift, Kate. No expectations attached. I just saw it and thought of Laurie."

My heart caught in my throat, and I glanced from Hank to my mom to Galigani to Laurie.

Laurie let out a gurgle of wonder as she held onto the neck of the rocking horse. Hank picked her up and gently set her on the saddle, keeping a steady hand on her back and rocking her. Laurie let out a gleeful shriek.

Galigani stalked back to his chair in the corner, steaming.

We let Laurie ride the horse for a few minutes, and then I announced it was time to head home.

"I'll help you load the horse into your car," said Hank.

I politely thanked him and gathered up Laurie and the diaper bag. Laurie cried out in anger when I pulled her off the horse. With a little grunt of frustration, I dug in the diaper bag for her stuffed duck, pulling it out in triumph. She wasn't totally satisfied, but she chewed on one of its wings, mollified enough to not throw a temper tantrum.

When we returned to the lobby, I pulled up short. *What's Kenny doing here?*

Besides leaning casually against the desk, talking to Odette, that is.

"I didn't schedule you to watch Laurie today, did I?" I called.

He glanced at me, looking startled and almost a little embarrassed. "Oh! Hey, Kate. No, I'm just here to meet Odette." He grinned at Odette and said to her, "So, I'll pick you up at seven?"

I'll pick you up at seven? They were going on a date? After I told her he was practically in high school?

I headed out into the parking lot, fuming under my breath. "I cannot believe them," I muttered.

"Why not, dear?" asked Mom.

"They can't go out on a date!" I said, opening the car door and buckling Laurie in. "He's eighteen. There's like a seven-year age gap."

Mom glanced back at the studio as Hank loaded the rocking horse in my car. "That's a big gap right now," she said, "but he's an adult, and you can't stop him."

"You sound like Jim," I grumbled.

"It probably won't last. And if it does, in three years, it won't be such an eye-raising age gap, and in five years, no one will think anything of it," she added.

I closed the car door. "Why not just book their wedding venue while we're at it?"

"Do you have anything against the girl, besides her age?" Hank asked.

Besides her age and her impossible elegance and the fact that Kenny's puppy love was making him an unreliable babysitter?

The truth sat in my throat like a bitter pill. I didn't really have anything against Odette. Nothing substantive. I'd just never seen Kenny fall so hard and so fast—he'd had a revolving door of crushes in the time I'd known him—and I was worried about what it meant for our family. I was being selfish. He was such a good, dependable babysitter, and I didn't want to lose him to a whirlwind romance.

But Kenny wouldn't be Laurie's babysitter forever. He was going to go to college and probably tour the world playing tuba professionally.

"No," I said finally. "She seems nice. I just worry about him."

I said goodbye to Mom and Hank—I wasn't sure where Galigani had gone—and drove home. Jim's car was already in the driveway, and so was Jo-Jo's truck. When I walked inside, I braced myself for the faint scent of sewage, but instead, the house smelled of taco seasoning. I took a deep breath. *So* much better than zombie diapers.

"Hey!" I called.

"Hey, honey!" Jim called from the kitchen.

I carried Laurie in and found Jim browning a pan of hamburger. The dishwasher was humming, and a bowl of chopped onions sat next to the stove.

Oh, how I loved that man. I planted a kiss on his cheek. "Thanks for making dinner! How was your day?"

Above the occasional sound of pounding from the garage, Jim told me about his client meetings—he'd landed another contract with the film studio he'd been working for—and I told him about our plans for the fundraiser and the awkward situation with Hank and Galigani.

He washed his hands and said, "Oh, should I bring the rocking horse in?"

I took over browning the meat, and a minute later, Jim had put the rocking horse on the kitchen floor and set Laurie on top of it. She squealed in delight.

"This is beautiful," Jim said. "Hank must really like your mom, huh?"

"I think he does," I said. "And he seems like a very nice guy. I just don't want Galigani to get hurt. Keep a hand on Laurie while she's on that thing, will you? I'm not sure she'll reliably keep her own balance."

When I went to the fridge to pull out a tomato and the block of cheddar cheese, I spied what looked like a tool sitting on the coffee table in the living room.

What on earth?

I set the food on the counter and went to investigate. Sure enough, there was a flat-head screwdriver just sitting on the coffee table. "Jim!" I yelled. "We can't leave tools out. Laurie is picking things up now. She could really hurt herself!"

"What do you mean?" he called from the kitchen.

I grabbed the screwdriver and stalked back to show it to him.

Jim's eyebrows ruffled. "That's not ours. Our screwdrivers are both red."

The handle on this screwdriver was undeniably black.

"Then how . . ." *Jo-Jo.*

The answer seemed to hit us both at the same time. Jim sighed and stood, picking up Laurie. "I'll go talk to him. When I got home, he came into the living room to tell me about something with the wiring, and he must have set down the screwdriver. Paula did say he could be forgetful."

"Yeah, you better talk to him," I muttered as Jim headed off to the garage with Laurie. "Because between pregnancy hormones and mama-bear instincts, I'm not going to be able to be nice."

CHAPTER 9

Jim assured me that Jo-Jo had apologized profusely and said it wouldn't happen again, and that he'd reiterated that the basement renovation would be *grand*.

"Thanks for talking to him about it." I smoothed the tablecloth onto the table. "Laurie's safe, and that's what counts."

While Jim finished setting the table, I texted Kenny to ask if he could watch Laurie the next day when I went to interview Kim and Todd.

We sat down to a taco salad dinner, and I fed Laurie little bites of cheese as we ate. Suddenly, the whole table seemed to shift. I grabbed Laurie's hand right before she tugged again at the tablecloth and brought all our dishes crashing down.

"Little duck!" I exclaimed. "That was a close one."

"What'd she do?" asked Jim.

"Pulled the tablecloth. Guess we'd better switch to placemats until she's older."

Jim chuckled. "I bet Whiskers would have appreciated taco salad on the floor."

"I've no doubt." I glanced down at Whiskers, who was staring at us mournfully. "She's trying to tell us she's never been fed in her whole life."

Jim took another bite of taco salad. "Little con artist."

When we finished dinner, Kenny still hadn't texted me back, so I called and left a message. With a sigh, I started making a list of everyone who was at the studio on the day of the murder. Best to do this comprehensively. Neither Galigani and I nor the police had come up with anything concrete. I needed to go over this with a fine-toothed comb to figure out what we'd missed.

People to interview:

1. *Kim*
2. *Todd—suspect in previous poisoning!*
3. *Odette*
4. *Kenny*
5. *Eddie*
6. *Dave*
7. *Petunia*

It was a start. Then I squinted at the list and added one more name.

1. *Monte—has motive!*

"No one saw anything that seemed suspicious," I mused to Jim, "although I haven't gotten to talk to Kim and Todd yet, because they've been dodging me. But I think it's time to dig deeper. Go over every last detail with them, to figure out something they might have seen that didn't strike them as important."

"Like I said"—Jim kissed my forehead—"you're the best PI in this town."

His praise made me feel warm and fuzzy, but I was secretly glad that I wasn't competing with Vicente Domingo on this case.

"I'm going to do a little case research tonight," I said. "There's a lead I want to get some background info on."

"I'll watch Laurie," said Jim.

Laurie, it turned out, wanted nothing more than to play on the rocking horse, so Jim kept one hand on her back while working on a design project on his laptop. I set up at the table and went to work, searching Google for any news references to the poisoning that Galigani told me Todd had allegedly been involved with.

There! An article from New York, dated twelve years earlier. There wasn't a whole lot of detail—it didn't even name Todd because he was a minor—but it did name the victim: nineteen-year-old Giselle Malakhova, who barely survived.

I researched the poison that had been used on Giselle, but it had been some sort of pesticide, not vercuronium bromide. Still, that didn't exonerate Todd in Leo's poisoning. He may have used whatever he could get his hands on—or perhaps he'd realize it would be suspicious to use the same method twice.

The following morning, when Kenny hadn't texted me back, I negotiated more daddy-daughter time for Jim since he was working from home and I headed over to the dance studio.

When I walked in, Petunia Petal greeted me. "Hey," she said warmly, coming out from behind the front desk to give me a hug. "I didn't realize you were coming."

She wasn't wearing florals today, but her tunic and leggings were in soft pastels that evoked spring.

She's really leaning into that stage name.

"Interviewing Kim and Todd finally," I said. "They were at the studio the day Leo died." I glanced at my watch. "I'm a couple of minutes early—can I ask you a few more questions? I'm trying to see what we might have missed, so I'm looking for any details you can think of, even if they don't seem relevant."

"Sure," she said, returning to her seat behind the desk. "About the day of the murder?"

"Anything from that day," I said, "or anything related to the other strange incidents. First, was anyone else here in the studio that day, besides these people?" I rattled off the list I'd written.

"Well, students," said Petunia. "But the schedule was full of private lessons, no group classes, and they were all kids, so I doubt they'd be involved."

"What about their parents?"

Petunia frowned in thought. "The kids were mostly dropped off. I can only think of one mom who stayed, and I visited with her the whole time. Oh! Hank did come by. He asked if your mom was here."

Hank, huh? He *was* a pharmacist. Who knew what concoctions he had behind the counter? I added another line to my list:

1. *Hank—might have access to poison?*

I tapped my pen against the legal pad. "Can you think of anyone who might want the fundraiser canceled? Anyone at all, no matter how petty the reason might be."

Petunia's mouth twitched. "I mean, other studios, I guess. Or maybe one of the teachers has an enemy. The dance world can be . . . competitive." Then she sighed. "Even if we don't cancel, do you think anyone will even come? It hit the newspaper, and that's terrible publicity."

A teenage girl in a leotard emerged from the hall, pointe shoes swung over her shoulder.

Petunia waved at her. "Bye, hon!"

"Bye, Miss Petal!" called the girl as she shoved her way through the door.

Petunia jerked her head toward the hall. "Kim and Todd are free now if you want to talk to them."

"Great! I have a few more questions for you, so I'll track you down later. But I haven't been able to do *any* interviews with them yet."

When I reached the dance room at the far end, I tapped on the doorframe. Todd totally ignored me, but Kim looked up with an annoyed expression. "Can I help you?"

"We had an appointment?" I raised my eyebrows.

"Oh. Right," said Kim. "Come in, I guess."

I grabbed one of the chairs at the back of the room and pulled it toward them. As I sat down, I asked, "So, you were here the day Leo died, right?"

"Yeah," said Kim, popping a stick of gum in her mouth. "Teaching classes."

"Did you see anything out of the ordinary?"

Todd sighed and looked at me for the first time since I'd entered the room. "We already answered all these questions for the police."

"Humor me." I kept my voice level and unbothered. "I'm trying to figure out if there's any clue we haven't unearthed yet." No need to let on that I knew about his high school poison escapades. I didn't want to tip my hand yet.

Though they answered my questions, each reply was short and abrupt, and they certainly weren't giving me anything helpful.

Todd's phone rang, and I thought I recognized the ringtone as something from *The Nutcracker*. He answered, and Kim took the opportunity to excuse herself to use the restroom.

"Yeah?" said Todd into the phone. He glanced at me and walked away, into the hall.

As soon as he disappeared from view, I stood and crept quietly toward the door. Staying just inside the room, I listened intently.

"Double the signing bonus, and you have a deal," said Todd. "I want to jump this ship." There was a long pause. "Yeah, yeah. Monte, cool it. Do you want us to come teach at your studio or not?" Another pause. "I'm taking care of it. Yes, our students will follow us."

Well, well, well. Todd *and* Monte had just skyrocketed to the very top of my list.

Todd hung up, but I didn't budge from where I was standing. He came through the door and stopped dead in his tracks.

I crossed my arms. "Want to tell me what that was all about?"

With a scowl, he spat, "None of your business."

"Sounded like you're going to sign with a competing studio and poach all of *Tre Fratelli Danzanti's* ballet students," I said. "And it also sounds like you're 'taking care' of something. That wouldn't have anything to do with Leo's death, now, would it?"

"No!" exclaimed Kim as she ran into the room. "Why would you think that?"

Todd brushed past me. "You took half a conversation out of context. We're not leaving *Tre Fratelli Danzanti*."

Kim's lips tightened into a thin white line.

"Would you like to clarify that, Kim?" I asked. "Because from where I stand, there are a lot of things not adding up. Especially since Todd has poisoned someone before."

Todd whirled on me, his face pale and trembling. "Who told you that?" he hissed. "I never poisoned anyone. Ever. My crazy ex-girlfriend lied. She said I poisoned Giselle for her in high school, but I didn't know anything about it."

"Why should I believe you? Give me something solid."

"Wait!" cried Kim. "We've talked about leaving the studio, but I don't want to go. We have a good gig here, and I don't trust Monte. Petunia's stuck up, but she treats us right."

Petunia, stuck up? That was rich, coming from Kim.

Todd scowled at Kim. "It's a twenty percent pay raise."

"Hold up," I said, "where were you guys the morning Leo was killed?"

"Here," said Todd, "you know that. That's why you were in here asking us questions."

"But where exactly?" I asked.

"In this room," he said, his palms facing upward. "Teaching."

"Did you have students every hour?"

He fell silent.

Kim answered, "Except between ten and eleven."

"Where were you between ten and eleven?" I asked.

"We stayed here," said Kim. "Putting together some choreography for our students."

"Can anyone else vouch for that?" I asked.

Desperation flashed across Kim's face. "Petunia, maybe, if she remembers passing us when she went back and forth between the office and the lobby. Listen, I don't know how to prove this, but we didn't do it."

"Can I have a phone number in case I have any more questions?"

With a subdued expression on her face, she rattled off her number and I programmed it into my phone. I left, considering the interaction. They were suspicious, but my gut said they didn't do it. Or at least that Kim wasn't involved. Todd was an open question. I still found him pretty suspicious.

Even if he wasn't a killer, he was slimy.

Of course, I still needed to follow up on everyone else and run down every clue I had. Next up, Petunia. Then, Odette.

CHAPTER 10

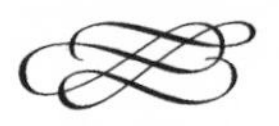

A couple dance teachers I didn't recognize were teaching ballroom classes, but I didn't see Odette. I found Petunia, jotted down the answers to a few more questions, and then asked when Odette would be in.

"Mmm, she was scheduled for a private lesson," Petunia said, "but the student canceled, so Odette took off with Kenny to film that music video."

"Do you know where they went?" I asked, shifting my purse to my other shoulder.

"Legion of Honor," she said. "I think they wanted to get some footage in front with the Thinker for that video their working on."

I climbed in my car and had just buckled my seatbelt when Jim called. "Hey, hon," he said, sounding excited. "How's the investigation going?"

"I have some interesting leads," I said. "Just about to take off to find Kenny and Odette."

"Oh! Good! Can you swing by the house and grab Laurie? I have a conference call in about forty minutes, and I thought it'd be fine to do it from the house, but Jo-Jo is making such a racket in the garage and it's going to be hard to balance Laurie and a work phone call from a library conference room."

"Yeah, definitely," I said. "Petunia told me Kenny's at the Legion of Honor. And the weather is so nice today, I'll take Laurie over to the playground near there. She'll love the swings."

I texted Kenny, *Where r u?* Then, not expecting an answer, I put the car in gear and headed off toward home. It took me a few minutes to gather Laurie, the diaper bag, and her sand pail—Jim was right, Jo-Jo was either working some sort of power drill or had let loose a nest of monster murder hornets in the garage—and by the time I left the house, Kenny hadn't texted me back. I called. No answer.

Well, hopefully I'd find them in front of the Legion of Honor museum. I snagged a parking spot near the fountain and bundled Laurie into the stroller. It was a beautiful, sunny day, but an unexpected chill cut through the air. We walked past the fountain, and I spotted Kenny slumped against one of the off-white pillars that made up the building's neoclassical front. He was wearing a sparkly silver shirt with the sleeves rolled up, a thin blue tie, and black pants.

Odette was nowhere in sight.

"Kenny!" I waved at him.

He glanced up, his confusion evident. "Kate? Laurie?"

A giggle gurgled out of Laurie when she heard Kenny's voice, and she squirmed in the stroller. When I reached Kenny, I pulled Laurie out, and she reached for him. He took her with a gentle smile, but seemed a little defensive when he looked back at me.

"What's up, Kate?"

"Petunia said I could find Odette here. I'm trying to go over everyone's statements again carefully and see what I may have missed."

Kenny's mouth opened and then closed. After a long pause, he said stiffly, "You don't . . . think she's a suspect, do you? I told you, I was with her the whole morning."

"I'm interviewing everyone again," I said in a soothing voice. "Not just people I suspect—"

"So, you *do* suspect her."

"I mean, I haven't ruled her out—"

"She couldn't have done it!" he said, annoyance flashing across his face.

I held up my hands and spoke in my most reassuring voice. "But mostly I'm here to see if there's anything else she might be able to remember, any detail, no matter how small, that she didn't think was significant. Something that might help me crack open the case."

This seemed to mollify Kenny a little, but he still looked petulant.

"Where is Odette, by the way?" I asked.

"She went in to use the restroom."

I studied Kenny. I'd never seen this kind of attitude out of him. That girl was no good for him.

Thirty seconds later, Odette emerged from the museum, decked out in a ruffly 1980s ballroom dress that matched the exact shade of Kenny's tie. Her eyebrows knitted in confusion when she saw me. "Hey, Kate," she said. "Did you decide to bring Laurie to the museum?"

The Legion of Honor wasn't exactly a children's museum, so I didn't blame her for being confused. "No, we're going to the playground at Lincoln Par, but Petunia said I could find you here. So, I thought I'd kill two birds, so to speak." I pulled my legal pad out of the stroller. "I'm tracking down everyone who was there the day of the murder to see if we can pick out any details that got missed the first time around. Anything you've realized you forgot to mention, or that didn't seem like a big deal at the time."

Odette shifted uncomfortably. "I mean, there's not much I can say, because I was really only there when Kenny and I came to get the costumes."

"Was anyone there who wasn't normally there? Or anyone missing who *was* normally there?"

Her nose twitched, and she shifted her weight from foot to foot. "I wasn't paying that close of attention. We went straight to the costume closet, and everything's a blur after . . . after we found Leo."

My face softened. "I'm sorry you had to see that. How are you doing?"

She took a deep, shaky breath. "It's hard."

"Were you guys here at the Legion of Honor that day? Filming, maybe, before you went to the studio?"

"Oh, no," said Odette. "We were just choreographing. We weren't filming yet. We were going to do some filming in the afternoon after we found costumes, but . . ."

"Everyone's plans got derailed," I said when she trailed off.

"You could say that."

"What time did you meet Kenny that morning?"

Odette's eyes darted to Kenny, then back to me. "Um, about eight, I think. We set the meeting for eight. I was a few minutes late."

I jotted down a note.

She squinted at my notetaking. "I mean, not late, late, just a couple minutes. Maybe five minutes or so."

I nodded. "Sure. Where were you before that?"

"I came straight from my apartment. You can ask my roommate to confirm."

I got her roommate's contact information, and then continued, "And you were with Kenny the whole day?"

She glanced at Kenny again. "Yeah. We were together all day." She shrugged. "Except, restroom breaks. And I got coffee," she added hurriedly. "But it was quick."

"And where were you choreographing?"

She gave the address of a park that was close to the studio, and added, "It's about halfway between work and home for me, and the gazebo actually makes for a pretty good dance floor."

"Why not choreograph at the studio?" I asked.

"Kate!" Kenny practically exploded. "I told you, she was with me the whole time. Seriously."

What in the world is wrong with him?

I frowned at Kenny, but moved quickly on from questions about the murder. Odette said she really couldn't think of anything else she'd noticed on the day of the burglary or from when the dead bird was left in the studio and that she hadn't even known about the hole in the roof. After hitting nothing but dead ends, I put Laurie back in stroller and waved goodbye to Odette and Kenny, feeling deflated.

When I reached the car, I turned back and looked at them. They were dancing some sort of intense ballroom dance—pasodoble? Argentine tango? I couldn't remember what was what. Whichever one was supposed to mimic a bullfight. *Pasodoble,* I decided. Kenny's phone was set up on a little tripod, filming them.

Kenny was right. He held his own. They looked great.

But I couldn't shake the feeling that something didn't add up. Odette hadn't seemed certain when she was giving her answers, like she was hoping she was confirming whatever Kenny had already told me. And it was *very* unlike Kenny to be so defensive.

"Another thing to follow up on, peannutty pie," I said to Laurie. "But for now, let's go find that swing set."

I pushed her stroller on the quick hike from the Legion of Honor to Lincoln Park, breathing in the fresh air and admiring my favorite view of the Golden Gate Bridge.

Once I strapped Laurie into the baby swing, I dialed Galigani.

"Hey, kid," he answered.

I brough him up to date, and then tacked on, "Oh, and Petunia mentioned that Hank swung by that day." I left out the reason Hank had stopped by. No need to raise Galigani's jealousy hackles.

There was a long pause. "Hank, huh?"

"He seems like a long shot, though. What would his motive be?" I moved from the back of the swing to the front and saw that Laurie's eyes were growing heavy-lidded.

"Well . . . I hate to say this, but—"

I doubt very much he hates to say it.

"—I did a little background research on Hank, and it turns out he knew Leo. Did he ever let on about that to you?"

He knew Leo? Weird.

I thought about the question while gently pushing Laurie, but I was certain this was new information. "He didn't say anything about it. Were they close?"

"They were part of a regular poker night."

"Poker? Did Hank owe Leo money?"

A group of moms with toddlers streamed into the park, one toddler making a bee-line for the swing set where I stood. Laurie jolted out of her rhythm induced stupor and chortled at the child.

"That's something we should find out," said Galigani grimly. "I got a tip that there might be some bad blood."

"And he's a pharmacist," I said, pulling Laurie out of the swing and giving the next child a turn.

"He'd know how to poison someone," Galigani said.

The silence hung heavy between us, and I stammered, "I-I'll head home now. I'll let you know when Jim gets back, and we can go talk to Hank together."

As I buckled Laurie back into her stroller, I tried to imagine how my next conversation with my mom was going to go. *Yeah, I believed your boyfriend when he said he thought your other boyfriend might be a murderer, and we went to interrogate him together.*

She and Kenny could commiserate, no doubt.

When I got home Jim was there, I only told him that Laurie was good and ready for a long nap, and I needed to go with Galigani to ask someone a few questions. I'd hear no end of the lectures if he thought I was letting my feelings about Mom and Hank and Galigani interfere with the case.

But I wasn't. It was a good lead. Motive plus means plus opportunity? Hank was lucky the cops hadn't hauled him in.

I met Galigani outside Hank's pharmacy. The smirk on Galigani's face looked entirely too smug.

"We don't *want* it to be him," I reminded him.

"Oh, of course not," said Galigani, his voice flat. "Your mom would be devastated."

With a warning glare, I marched inside, Galigani trailing me.

A twentysomething pharmacy tech stood behind the counter. "Can I help you?" he asked.

"Hank here?" Galigani practically held his breath.

The tech nodded and twisted to call toward the back, "Hey, Hank. Visitors for ya!"

Hank came around the corner, wearing a white coat. He brightened when he saw me, but then he took in Galigani, and his lips tightened into a thin line. "Good to see you both."

Galigani whipped out a notepad and pen, looking coldly officious. I was pretty sure it was a deliberate move to intimidate Hank. "Can we ask you a few questions about the murder of Leo Godwin?"

Hank blinked several times. "Sure," he said slowly, glancing at the open-mouthed pharmacy tech. "Although I don't know what I can help you out with. Should we do this over dinner?"

"Why not?" Galigani gestured to the door. "After you."

We grabbed burgers at the place next door, and Galigani started the questioning. "Where were you the morning of the tenth?"

"Well," Hank wiped a dab of ketchup off his lip, "here most of the day. When it was slow, I went over to *Tre Fratelli Danzanti* to see if Vera might be there."

Galigani paused, his lips quirked in irritation. "And why did you think Vera might be there?"

"Well, she needs a dance partner, and she'd mentioned she might be there pretty often to help out with the fundraiser."

Galigani practically exploded. "She doesn't need a dance partner who's a murderer!"

CHAPTER 11

We can't just go accusing people without evidence. I rested a gentle hand on Galigani's arm. He was a better PI than this. But jealousy did crazy things to a person. I'd almost lost my mind when Jim's ex-girlfriend tried to drive us apart.

"What he means," I said in Hank's direction, "is that we're trying to follow up with anyone who was at *Tre Fratelli Danzanti* that morning. Not"—I glared at Galigani—"because we're accusing anyone of anything, but because we're looking for leads. Anything you might have noticed that seemed odd, or that stands out now that you think back on it."

Hank chewed slowly on a bite of burger. When he swallowed, he said, "I wasn't there very long, really. Don't remember much. Of course, I was looking for Vera, not paying attention to all the goings-on at the studio."

"Why didn't you just call her?" I asked.

He shifted in his seat, and a faint blush crept over his face. "She would have hung up on me. We'd talked on the phone the night before, and she told me she was already in love with someone and that we should just be friends. I tried to talk her out of it—"

Galigani fumed. "Why, you no-good—"

I cut him off by clamping a hand on his shoulder. "That's

wonderful news!" I overenunciated each word, hoping to get it through Galigani's thick skull. "Mom is in love with someone else. That must make her boyfriend very happy."

Galigani's mouth closed as the realization hit him.

Ignoring the jubilation emanating from my mentor, I looked back at Hank. "So, you were hoping to run into her and . . ."

"Apologize for not respecting her wishes the evening before, and tell her I'd be happy to be her platonic dance partner for the fundraiser."

Galigani's face took on a sour expression again. I couldn't blame him for being a little possessive. "And so now you're showering her granddaughter with expensive gifts?"

Hank shrugged. "A man's gotta try."

"Did you know Leo?" I asked before Galigani could retort a reply.

He popped a fry in his mouth with an expression of distaste. "I met him while taking dance lessons there a year or two back. We saw each other at poker on occasion."

"Anyone owe him money?"

Hank shook his head. "We didn't play for that much. I expect there were some outstanding debts—maybe involving Leo, maybe not—but nothing anyone would kill over. Two or three hundred dollars tops."

None of our specific questions about who he'd seen at the studio yielded anything. He knew he'd seen Petunia because she'd told him that Vera wasn't there. But he hadn't registered anyone else, or what cars were parked nearby, or anything useful.

When we stood to leave, I leaned forward and said, "Hey, I really don't mean anything by this, but could you stay in town in case we have any more questions? I know you travel a lot, and I want to make sure we rule you out before the police get wind of that poker night."

"Sure, sure." He tossed the hamburger wrapper in the bin. "I don't have plans to go anywhere."

Galigani and I walked to his car. "Should we go see if we can track down Todd now?" he asked.

"Sounds great. You driving?"

"Yep."

As soon as the car doors closed, I asked, "So, what'd you think of Hank's story?"

He made a scoffing noise in his throat. "Well, I believed the part about your mother being in love with me."

"Really? That's what you're leading with? We're on a case!"

"*You're* on a case," he said. "I'm retired, you know, but somehow you always rope me back in."

"As my supervisor, you're definitely also working this case."

"As your supervisor, I'm somehow not going to see a dime from this case," he muttered.

He had a point. I drummed my fingers on the armrest.

"To be consistent," he continued, "we really should view Petunia and the owners as suspects."

"I know, I know," I sighed. "Just because I know them doesn't mean I can rule them out. I know they didn't do it, but it's important to dot all my *i*'s and cross all my *t*'s and all that."

"Yes, *and all that*," he said, mimicking me.

I laughed aloud, and he joined me, chuckling.

"Galigani, you are ornery today."

"Why, Kate, I'm always ornery. You just happened to notice today."

My stomach growled. "Can we stop off for stakeout snacks before we go to the studio to wait for Todd? I'm famished."

* * *

"BINGO," CRIED GALIGANI THREE HOURS LATER, PEERING THROUGH HIS binoculars at the studio. "Todd and Kim, and they're going to separate cars. They live together, don't they? Do you think there's trouble in paradise?"

"I hope so," I said, crunching into a potato chip. "Kim could do better."

"I thought you said they were both snobs." He put the car in gear.

"Well, they *are* both snobs. But Todd wants to betray Dave and Petunia, and Kim doesn't, so that makes her a better person in my book. Plus, as far as we know, she's never poisoned anyone."

"Well, Todd says he hasn't poisoned anyone either." Galigani put the car back in park. "Hey, he's not leaving after all. He was just loading some stuff in his car."

I grabbed the binoculars and zoomed in on Todd. "He's headed over to Monte's studio. Traitor." Unbuckling my seatbelt, I said, "I'll follow him in. See if I can overhear anything. If he sees me, I'll just say I'm there to ask Monte questions."

With a gruff nod, Galigani said, "Be careful, kid."

"I'm always careful. Besides, I owe you a ring-shopping trip. Especially now that we have it on good authority that Mom is"—I dramatically fluttered my hand over my chest—"in love."

Galigani's cheeks pinked. "Shut up, and go investigate," he growled. But he couldn't fool me. He was trying and failing to keep a silly grin off his face.

"I call matron of honor," I said right before I closed the door. Shivering, I strode across the shaded parking lot, wishing I'd brought my sweater. But no time to go back for it. Who knew how long Todd would be at Monte's?

The lobby of Dare to Dance looked similar to *Tre Fratelli Danzanti's,* except instead of a quote stenciled on the wall, there were huge posters of professional dancers. A few were ballroom, but it seemed like this studio was more ballet-centric than Dave's. Male voices emanated from behind a half-open door just off the lobby. The office, I bet. I crept closer, keeping myself out of the eyesight of anyone within.

Yes, I decided as I listened to the tenor of the voices. *Todd and Monte for sure.*

"Listen, I did what you asked," Todd said, frustration lacing his voice.

"I heard." Monte seemed to be shuffling some papers. "I'll get you a healthy bonus."

"Thanks," said Todd. "My mom's short some money for her medical bills . . ."

The ensuing silence seemed awkward, and I pulled out my phone and texted Galigani. *Todd says he did what Monte asked and is getting a bonus.*

I sent it, then hurried to put my phone on silent so Todd and Monte wouldn't hear when Galigani replied.

His text came quickly. *I've called the police. They'll want to ask some questions about that.*

Todd and Monte were speaking more quietly now, hashing out details of the transition—Todd and Kim were both going to teach ballet for Monte.

What nerve!

When the first two cops strode in, I was relieved—and when I saw Deb's face, I grinned. "Hey," I said, high-fiving her. "I got something for you."

"So I hear. Good work, Connolly."

Todd and Monte came out of the office, their arms crossed.

"What's this about?" demanded Todd.

"We've received some information connecting you with a local homicide. I'm afraid we're going to take you down to the station for questioning," said Deb.

"What!" Monte fumed.

Todd glared in my direction. "I knew you were going to be trouble."

I shrugged. "You want to tell us what 'I did what you asked' and 'I'll get you a healthy bonus' means? Because that sounds pretty suspicious when someone's sabotaging Todd's boss and one of his coworkers ends up dead."

"We're not going anywhere," growled Monte. Another patrol unit pulled in front of the studio and Monte roared even louder, "Hey now! This is a respectable establishment. You're going to ruin my reputation!"

"Maybe then just come down for the station for a friendly chat," Deb said with a cheery grin.

Todd shook his head and held up his hands. "Listen, it's not what you think. We didn't hurt anyone. We just—"

Monte bustled ahead of Todd out the door. "Let's save it for the station," Monte said. "My lawyer will meet us there."

Todd trained his eyes on me. "Really, Kate. It's not what you think."

The cops led him out, and I shivered. Maybe he was guilty, maybe he wasn't, but I was glad he was being taken in for questioning.

Galigani and I followed them out, and then Deb jogged back to meet us and whispered, "I'll let you know what we find out."

The police cars pulled away, and Galigani and I both let out deep breaths.

"Pretty full PI day, huh?" he said. "I was going to ask if we could go by the mall to look at rings, but I'm exhausted and you must be too."

I cradled my baby bump. Second trimester or not, I *was* exhausted. Suddenly, I wanted nothing more than to be home, cuddled in bed with Jim and Laurie.

"If you end up browsing before we find time to go together," I said, "remember that Mom likes sparkly things but has small hands. Big diamonds look ridiculous on her. She'll be happiest with something that looks intricate but has a thin band and a center diamond no bigger than three-quarters of a carat."

Galigani jotted down a note with those specifications, and we agreed to touch base the next day to talk about where we were in the case.

A profound sense of relief filled me as I pulled into the driveway. Jo-Jo's truck wasn't anywhere in sight. It would be a quiet evening at home.

Jim had just finished feeding Laurie, and she grinned when she saw me.

"How is my peanuty pie?" I cooed. I scooped her up and planted kisses on her tummy.

"Ready for our dance lesson tomorrow?" Jim asked. "I scheduled it for the morning because my day is wide open."

"Oh, I'm ready," I said in a teasing voice. "The question is if you're ready."

Jim clutched a hand to his chest as if affronted. "Ouch! Listen, I've just misplaced my rhythm, I'm sure it's here somewhere and I'll find it."

Snorting, I said, "Have you checked for under the couch?"

Jim laughed. "Yeah. Unfortunately, my rhythm isn't there."

We both chucked, and Laurie let out a high-pitch delighted squeal.

I kissed the top of her head, my heart warmed with love for my little family.

Jim regained his serious expression, and said, "And check the table. We got some packages today. I think maybe the baby-proofing stuff."

"Good! Let's get that installed in the next few days. She's grabbing ahold of everything, and she may start crawling soon."

"You can say that three times fast," said Jim, shuddering. "I set her down for just a second and she almost spilled coffee on my laptop."

"Imagine when she's mobile."

He shook his head. "We're going to have our work cut out for us for sure. So, how was the investigating? Find out anything good?"

Setting Laurie on the rocking horse and sitting on the living room carpet beside her, I thought of Hank, and guilt churned in my belly. Really, I didn't want him to be guilty. "Talked to a few suspects. A couple of guys got pulled in for questioning. That guy ballet teacher and the owner of the rival studio. I think they may have been working together."

"What's the motive?" asked Jim, settling onto the couch.

I leaned my head against his leg. "Well, for the owner, sabotaging Dave's studio and poaching his clients. Expanding his business and eventually taking over Dave's unit. For the teacher . . . it sounds like he's in some financial trouble. Or his mom is. Medical bills."

"Yikes," said Jim. "That's sad when you think about it."

"Well," I traced my fingers over the rocking horse head, "we don't have anything concrete yet."

We settled into an easy silence, and Jim said, "Such a beautiful gift from Hank."

"It is. Laurie sure loves it. And it's way better than that howling chipmunk bus."

Jim chuckled, then joined me sitting on the floor. He kissed me until we fell back onto the carpet laughing.

CHAPTER 12

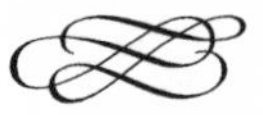

o Do

1. Follow up with Deb on Monte/Todd interrogation.
2. Tell Dave that Todd is scheming to poach students.
3. Ring shopping with Galigani!
4. Install baby-proofing system.
5. Dance lesson! Is it too soon to sign Laurie up ballet?
6. Meet with Petunia about fundraiser.

AN OPPRESSIVE POUNDING SOUND TUGGED AT THE EDGES OF MY consciousness. I groaned and rolled over, trying to maintain the perfect relaxation of sleep.

But then a shrill sound cut through the drumbeat of Jo-Jo's construction work. Laurie was crying. He'd woken her up too. I grumbled but clambered out of bed, keeping my eyes closed. My feet traced the pathway to her room by sheer muscle memory.

"Hey, peanut." I cracked one eye open and pulled her out of her crib. "Should we feed you?"

We returned to the bedroom I shared with Jim, and I climbed back under the covers with her and positioned her to nurse. Her squalls settled almost immediately, and I scooted backward so that my back touched Jim. This was a perfect morning.

The obnoxious drone of a power tool replaced the pounding that had first woken me.

Well, almost perfect. "It'll be over soon," I whispered to Laurie. "He'll finish all the work and we'll have a perfect nursery for the twins. And you'll be the world's best big sister."

Was that coming from the backyard? Why the heck was Jo-Jo working in the backyard?

Plus, it wasn't yet seven—why did Jo-Jo have to start his work so darn early? I let myself hover between wakefulness and sleep while Laurie finished nursing. When she was done eating, I forced myself to fully wake up. I stood, craning my neck to stretch out the tense muscles. "We should change your diaper, huh?"

Jim stirred in bed, and I called, "Can you make some coffee? I'll just have half a cup. I need a kickstart this morning."

He sat up, yawning. "Sure, sure."

I took Laurie back to her ducky-themed nursery while Jim padded down the hall to the kitchen. The sound of the coffee maker and the promise of even the tiniest bit of caffeine from our decaf brew perked me up. Someday the nursery would be done, and we wouldn't be woken up so early. Of course, the twins would keep us up at all hours of the night—but at least I wouldn't be pregnant and I could start drinking a reasonable amount of coffee again.

I glanced at my phone, wondering when I could expect a call from Deb. Maybe I'd text her. I opened my text messages and saw she'd texted me at two in the morning.

Girl we need to do a GIRLS NIGHT SOON. I LOVE YOU!

Judging from that text, I shouldn't expect a call anytime soon—no doubt Deb would sleep late and wake up nursing a giant hangover. I sighed. Sometimes I worried about her.

Instead, I texted Galigani, *Can you find out anything from your contacts at the station? Deb out of commission with a migraine.*

Galigani used to be on the police force, so his contacts were broader and deeper than mine. He'd encouraged me to foster relationships with some of the cops so that I'd have a proper network when I got my PI license and he truly retired.

Maybe I should spend some time getting to know Jones and his wife. They had a kid not much older than Laurie, and it'd be nice to have more than one contact feeding me information from the station.

And Nick, the ME. That was a relationship I wanted to foster too. Maybe I could find something Wonder Woman-themed for his wife. I added it to my list.

At 9:10, Galigani called, "Hey, kid, I got an update for you."

I grabbed my legal pad to take notes. "Go on."

"Todd and Monte's stories matched. They said Monte had been trying to get Todd and Kim to come work for him—something about taking most of *Tre Fratelli Danzanti's* ballet students—and that Todd had just earned a bonus by talking Kim into the plan. She was reluctant, I guess. Monte has a solid alibi for the morning of the murder, which is why he's never been high on the list of suspects."

"But he could have had someone else do his dirty work for him," I said, scribbling furiously.

"Yeah, he doesn't seem like the type to get his hands dirty," agreed Galigani. "But their story provides a reasonable explanation for the conversation you heard. We'll keep an eye on them, but it's a dead-end for now."

I sighed, rubbing my temples. "We're running out of time. The fundraiser is in less than a week, and someone else might die if we don't catch the killer by then."

"Well," said Galigani, "we'll just chase down the leads as we uncover them. 'Almost a week' may not sound like much time, but it's an eternity in the private investigation business."

Jim and I got ready for our lesson, and I decided on the same 1950s-style maternity dress I'd worn to our first lesson with Odette. At first, I wasn't going to do my hair and makeup, but when I looked in the mirror, I decided a little red lipstick couldn't hurt.

And eyeliner would really make the ensemble pop.

I glanced from my phone clock to my curling iron and back again. My hair was looking frizzy today, and I was pretty sure I had just enough time to tame it into perfect 1950s ringlets.

Samantha Spade, Private Eye was back in business.

Unfortunately, Kenny wasn't back in the babysitting business. He'd responded noncommittally the night before when I'd asked him about watching Laurie, and I didn't feel like chasing him down yet again. Paula and Mom were running around busy with preparations for the fundraiser, so we were just going to have to take Laurie and hope for the best.

On the way to the studio, Jim and I stopped off at a print shop to pick up the final printed flyers for the event—I triple-checked to make sure *public* was spelled right. "I'll hang these around town this afternoon and tomorrow," I said, patting the thick envelope. "We need to get the word out."

"The newspaper is doing quite a good job of getting the word out," said Jim. "They've run three stories about the murder and the upcoming fundraiser."

"Hope it's true that there's no such thing as bad publicity," I said.

Laurie banged her rattle against the plastic of her car seat, fussing.

"Even Laurie's worried about it." I snorted.

Jim chuckled.

"You're the marketing expert," I said. "What do you think?"

Laurie dropped her rattle. I twisted around to pick it up and return it to her. She clutched it with a soft coo.

Jim whistled, thinking. "I'd rather have bad publicity than no publicity, as a general rule. If the killer is caught before the event, I think it will help turn people out for it. If the killer is still on the loose, people might worry it's unsafe."

"Well, we have to catch the killer before then, anyway," I said, crossing my fingers for luck. "So no one else gets hurt."

When we walked into the lobby of *Tre Fratelli Danzanti,* Petunia announced she and Dave were taking over our lesson.

I set Laurie on the gleaming wood floor in the corner of the room, hoping her ducky and a couple of other toys would keep her occupied. It wasn't a perfect solution, but hopefully, it would give us at least some time to practice.

We started by reviewing the rock step and triple step, and then went back to the Charleston. I breathed deeply, maintaining awareness of my center of gravity, and executed every step perfectly.

Jim, on the other hand . . .

I glanced at Dave, who was wincing as he watched Jim attempt the Charleston. After a moment, Dave said, "Alright, what if we try it like this . . ."

It was no use. Even when Jim got the steps right—and he stepped wrong about half the time—he wasn't moving fluidly, and his face was all scrunched up from focusing too hard on the choreography.

And Dave wanted us to be exhibition-ready in a week?

It seemed like Dave and Petunia were thinking the same thing. "Well," said Petunia when we hit the halfway point, "I hope this doesn't come off the wrong way, but will you be comfortable having attention on your dancing at the fundraiser? It's nothing wrong with you!" Her words spilled out more quickly as she tried to spare his feelings. "But you just look like you're trying so hard, and I wonder if you'll be able to relax on the day of the fundraiser."

Jim nodded grimly. "I can do it. I'll help wherever you need me to help."

Dave and Petunia shared a long look, and finally, Dave burst out laughing. "I'm so sorry, Jim, I was actually making a joke when I said I wanted you to be part of the demonstration. Odette misunderstood, and when I found out she'd told you, I thought for sure you'd back out, and . . ."

Petunia's eyes widened in horror, and she elbowed Dave. "Be nice!" she hissed.

But Jim wasn't offended. His shoulders slumped in relief. "Oh, thank God. I didn't know what you were thinking, but I didn't want to let you down."

"Kate, on the other hand," said Petunia, "I think we could have you be an example for the beginners. Would you be interested in doing that?"

"Only if you're not making a joke," I answered with a wink.

"We're going to teach beginners five dance steps in the hour before the fundraiser officially starts," she said. "That'll help people who don't know much about dancing but who want to come to the event feel like they can dance a little, so they can relax and have fun."

Laurie started fussing, and Jim said happily, "I'll take care of her. Why don't you learn the other two steps?"

Dave grabbed me in his arms and twirled me around the floor.

"Wow, you make dancing so easy," I said.

He laughed. "Kate you a natural. Your only problem is you try to take the lead."

We burst out laughing and Petunia called out, "You guys look like you're having too much fun!"

"How's it going with the investigation?" Dave asked.

"Well, during the course of the investigation, I found out something you should know. Can we go to your office and chat?"

A shadow crossed Dave's face. "Of course. What is it?"

"Let's go to the office," I said. "Away from any listening ears."

I motioned for Petunia and Jim to follow us. We all settled into seats in the office, Dave and Petunia on one side of the desk and Jim and me on the other.

"Listen, we don't know for sure if this has anything to do with the murder or any of the other strange things that have been going on, but Todd and Kim aren't loyal to you."

"Shocker," muttered Petunia under her breath.

"What do you mean?" Dave asked.

"Monte's been trying to get them to come work for him," I explained, pulling my legal pad out of the diaper bag and flipping to the relevant page of notes. "He was offering them a pay raise, plus a cash bonus. Kim was more reluctant than Todd, but it sounds like Todd talked her into it."

"So, they're quitting?" Dave leaned back in his chair, looking perturbed.

"Not just quitting," I said with a sigh. This was the hardest part—no one wanted to hear that someone they knew was about to stab them in the back. Figuratively, in Dave's case.

Perhaps literally, in Leo's.

I continued, "Todd devised a plan with Monte to convince most of their ballet students to follow them to the new studio."

Dave blanched. "That's over half our revenue. We'd . . . we'll go under."

"That seems to have been part of Monte's plan." I bit my lip.

Dave shuffled the papers in front of him as if his hands needed to occupy themselves. "And Todd went along with this?"

"I'm sorry," I said gently. "I know it's hard to hear."

The door burst open, and Kim ran in, breathing heavily, her dark hair flying out behind her in a ponytail.

Dave studied her with an inscrutable expression, and Petunia just turned her attention to the paperwork on the desk.

Kim pulled up short when she saw Jim and me, but she addressed Dave. "Todd's leaving *Tre Fratelli Danzanti,* but I don't want to," she blurted, her lower lip trembling. "He kept telling me we needed to, that he needed the money to pay his mom's medical bills, and I'm sorry his mom is sick, but I can't do this."

CHAPTER 13

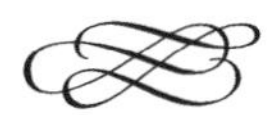

Dave's face softened as he gazed at Kim. "What changed? Kate says you agreed to leave and take the students with you. You have to know that would ruin us. We've worked hard building our client base."

Kim looked stricken. "He manipulated me into saying yes, but he lied. He said his mom needed a treatment that insurance wouldn't cover, but I found a letter at her apartment dated three weeks ago that said the treatment had been approved. I . . . I told him we were through. He can't lie to me like that. And worse—he did it for a payday."

I hazarded a glance at Petunia. She seemed thoughtful but guarded. Like she was trying to figure out whether to believe Kim or not.

"Why do you want to stay, Kim?" Petunia finally asked.

Kim looked down at the floor. "It's a good gig," she mumbled. "And you're always fair with us."

Petunia chewed her lip for a moment, then nodded as if satisfied.

Shifting from foot to foot—and still managing to look perfectly elegant—Kim said, "I can teach the classes myself. He tried to make me think I couldn't, but the students love me, and I know what I'm doing. He won't be able to take hardly any of the students if I don't go with him. Certainly no more than two or three."

They talked for a couple more minutes, but I let my mind wander. We hadn't absolutely cleared Todd, but I was starting to think it didn't add up. What would be the point of killing Leo? If Todd and Monte could halve *Tre Fratelli Danzanti's* revenue just by taking the ballet students, why escalate to murder?

"Kim," I said as she turned to leave, "I'm going to ask you something, and I need you to be completely honest with me."

She hesitated, then nodded.

"Did anyone at the studio know about Todd's plan to leave?"

Shaking her head, she said, "Not until you overheard Todd on the phone. I insisted he keep it totally secret. I . . . don't think he was sloppy when he let you overhear. He was running out of patience, and I think he wanted to force the issue. He wanted you to hear that phone conversation so that I'd be forced to stop delaying and make a choice. I'm so angry at him I can't see straight, but he's not a killer. I'd bet my life on it. I was with him the whole morning of the tenth."

I mentally crossed Todd and Kim off my list. It was possible that she was lying about all of this, that this was an elaborate ruse to deflect suspicion, but I didn't think so.

"Thank you," I said. "This was very helpful."

When the door closed behind her, Jim said, "Well, that resolved itself quickly, didn't it?" His phone buzzed, and he glanced at the screen. "Oh, that's a client," he said, handing Laurie off to me.

What I wouldn't give for a reliable babysitter. I bounced Laurie on my left knee and set my legal pad on the desk. Might as well ask about Hank. I couldn't come up with a solid motive for him, since I didn't have any evidence that gambling had caused problems between him and Leo. But means and opportunity made for a compelling case now that Todd and Monte didn't seem like high-priority suspects.

"Can you guys tell me about Hank's relationship with the studio?" I asked. "I'm just following up on everyone who was here that day."

"Sure," said Dave. "He's been in and out for a couple of years, I guess. Does that seem right, Petunia?"

"Yeah, I think so." She clicked and unclicked her pen. "I can look it up in our records."

"Small world that he knows your mom," said Dave.

With a chuckle, I said, "That's San Francisco for you."

Laurie grabbed my legal pad off the desk, and I pried it from her fingers and set it back down, out of her reach.

"Funny that you ask about him," Dave added, glancing at his phone screen. "He's going to be here later today to help Paula hang her decorations."

"Oh?" That came as a surprise, but he was probably hoping to talk to my mom. He'd said as much to Galigani and me.

"Hank's loaded," said Petunia in a conspiratorial whisper. "He'd be a nice catch for your mom."

I was unmoved. It didn't matter how rich Hank was, I was Team Galigani all the way. So I just responded with a polite smile.

"He gave us a loan about a year ago when we needed a little help covering payroll," said Dave. "We got that paid off, what, six months ago? He's a big lover of the arts. Supports local bands. Has his name on a box at the symphony. Invests in dance studios. That sort of thing."

Invests in dance studios? An idea started to form at the edges of my consciousness. What if . . .

Jim popped his head back in the office with an apologetic grimace. "Hey, Kate, can I take you and Laurie home now? That client just set up a meeting in an hour, and they want me there in person."

Frustration bubbled in my chest. If Jim couldn't watch Laurie, that meant I couldn't follow up on my hunch—it didn't feel safe to take my baby snooping around Monte's studio. But Jim's career was really taking off, and his meetings were an important part of that. So I plastered on a smile and said, "Yeah, definitely."

We ran into Paula in the parking lot on the way out. "Kate!" she called, hope lighting up her face. "Where are you off to?"

"Back home," I said. "You need me?"

She grinned. "Can I borrow your coat? I realized I left my sweater at home, and it is *cold* in the studio. They keep it a comfortable temperature for people who've been dancing for an hour."

I laughed and shrugged out of my black coat. It was two sizes too large for Paula, but somehow it looked effortlessly fabulous over her skinny jeans and peplum blouse.

"Hey, I kinda like this," she said, glancing down at it.

"I am *lending* it," I exclaimed. "I still remember how you stole my polka dot sweater in tenth grade."

"Borrowed . . . for an extended period of time," she corrected with a wink.

On the way home, I texted my mom to ask what she was up to.

Trying a new recipe, she replied. *How about I bring some over?*

Well, at least she wasn't planning to be at the studio while Hank was there. *Sounds great,* I typed.

What culinary shenanigans were in store for me? I was afraid to find out. But it couldn't be worse than savory popsicles.

Mom's recipe turned out to be an ambrosia salad—canned pineapple, canned mandarins, marshmallows, whipped cream, coconut, and a small army of maraschino cherries.

"You have to try it, dear," said Mom, setting the bowl on my counter. "It's quite good, if I do say so myself."

I eyed the concoction skeptically and shifted Laurie to my other hip. The 1950s was a great decade for lipstick, but an odd one for food.

Laurie did not share my cynicism. She plunged her hand into the bowl and helped herself to a slurping bite before I could react. She gnawed on her whipped-cream-covered hand with a contented gurgle.

Mom and I burst out laughing.

"Well, it's got one fan," I said, pulling a bowl down from the kitchen cabinet and helping myself to a scoop of the strange-looking dessert.

"Well?" asked Mom, anticipation written all over her face.

"Pretty good," I said as soon as I swallowed the first bite. "I like it more than the baked Alaska, actually."

We chatted as I ate, and I helped myself to a second serving.

"So," I said finally, "what's going on with you and Hank?"

"You know, same old, same old. Hanging out and having fun." She pulled out a bowl of her own and spooned some ambrosia salad into it.

Alarm bells rang in my head. What happened to Mom being in

love with Galigani and not wanting to date Hank? "What about Galigani?" I asked, trying to keep myself from sounding petulant.

"Well, I don't think Galigani wants anything too serious right now," said Mom.

"Have you asked him about that?"

We headed into the living room and settled on the couch. Mom took Laurie and set her on the rocking horse.

She didn't even notice that I'd hidden the howling chipmunk bus.

"We talked earlier today," said Mom, "and he's just fine with me seeing Hank some. I was disappointed at first—things have been going very well, and I thought we might be making something official soon—but then I realized he was right. There's no rush. Neither one of us are going anywhere."

Galigani said *what*? I was going to have to have a chat with him about that. But I decided to change the subject for now.

"Oh, did Hank mention to you that he knew Leo?" I asked casually. "He told me that when I went to ask him if he'd seen anything suspicious at the studio."

"What? Oh, yes. Poor Leo. They were part of the same guy's night, but they weren't really close."

I certainly wasn't going to let on to Mom that I was investigating Hank as a possible suspect. So I just said, "It still must have come as something of a shock. Is he doing all right?"

"He seems fine," said Mom, resting her hand on Laurie's back. "We're going to dinner tonight."

I gritted my teeth. "About tonight. Any way you can take Laurie for a couple hours? I have a good lead to chase down, and my childcare is evaporating faster than snow in LA."

"Hmm. Could you try to get back by five thirty? We're going to a nice restaurant."

"I will do my very best. Worst-case scenario, you can use the evening to complain about your ungrateful daughter who expects you to be free childcare."

Mom laughed and kissed Laurie's curls. "I'm always glad to spend time with this little munchkin, and you know it."

"Thank you!" I said. "You're the best."

Before I left, I touched up my red lipstick and tousled my curls. If I was going to snoop around on the same day as a dance class, I would definitely have a little fun feeling like a film noir detective.

I turned jazz music on in the car and drove to the studio. When I arrived, I decided to park on the *Tre Fratelli Danzanti* side and walk the short distance to Monte's. In my short career as a private investigator, I'd had a few incidents of suspects targeting me while I was driving. So, I figured it'd be best that Monte didn't see what kind of car I drove.

Holding my breath, I pushed open the door to Monte's studio. Like before, there was no one at the front desk. The office door had been left cracked open, and from the hallway, I could hear the sound of classical music. There must be a class going on somewhere in the back. I gently rapped on the office door. No answer.

Go time.

I stepped into the office. Sure enough, there was no one around. I sat down at the desk and clicked the computer mouse. The screen flashed to life. No password required.

If Monte was involved with something illegal, he sure was doing a bad job of keeping his information secure.

But I wasn't here to investigate Monte.

I found the office's accounting software and opened it up. Pulling up the reports, I searched for *Hank Henning*.

"Bingo!" I whispered.

Five months earlier, Hank had invested twenty thousand dollars in Monte's studio, buying a twenty-five percent stake.

That was motive. If *Tre Fratelli Danzanti* went out of business and Monte expanded into their space, Hank stood to make money.

Plus, it struck me as very, very odd that he hadn't disclosed his business relationship with Monte earlier.

"Well, Galigani," I whispered. "I might be about to make your day." I snapped photos of the screen, and heard the sound of voices in the hall. Heart pounding, I darted out of the office. No one in the lobby, but the voices were getting closer. It sounded like a class had just gotten out. I ran into the parking lot.

Home free.

And then relief evaporated, and my blood ran cold as I spotted someone lying face down in the parking lot.

I screamed and sprinted to the figure.

A figure I would have recognized anywhere. My best friend Paula lay still.

I shook her frantically, despair clutching my heart.

"Paula! Paula! Oh my Lord. Please! Paula!"

I was vaguely aware of a crowd gathering, someone calling help. I pressed my face wet with tears against Paula's and felt her breath on my cheek. I gasped. "Yes, girl. Yes. You keep breathing."

CHAPTER 14

I clutched Paula until the ambulance arrived. The paramedics tried to separate us, but I climbed into the back with her and wouldn't budge.

Halfway to the emergency room, she stirred.

"Paula!" I squeezed her hand. "Are you all right? What happened?"

She blinked a few times, her face pale and drawn. "Kate?" she asked slowly. "What . . . what happened?"

"I just asked you that, silly," I said, squeezing her fingers and affecting a chipper voice.

"Oh. I don't . . . remember."

I glanced at the paramedic, who shrugged and said, "Hazy memory is common after a head injury. It may come back to her, it may not."

"You're going to be fine, Paula." I brushed a strand of hair out of her face. "We're just on our way to the hospital to run some tests. It looks like you fell and hit your head. As soon as they've cleared you, we'll get you back home to Danny and Chloe."

After we arrived, they wheeled Paula back for a brain scan, and I paced her hospital room like an agitated raccoon.

"Darling!"

I whirled around to see Mom in the doorway. "Mom!" I rushed to her and crumpled into her embrace. "Paula's hurt—"

"I heard," she said, her usual dramatic manner subdued. "Petunia called me. How bad is it? Will she be okay?"

"I think so. She woke up. They're scanning for brain bleeds now." Then I stood up straight. "Where's Laurie?"

"With Kenny," said Mom serenely. "When I told him what happened, he dropped everything to come pick her up."

I let out a little sigh of relief. Twitterpated or not, Kenny really could be depended on in a crisis.

Mom led me to a chair. "He's performing in a show tonight, so you do need to get back to pick up Laurie soon. But first, sit down. You need to relax, dear."

"How can I relax?" I cried.

"Well, you may not be able to." She gently rubbed my shoulders. "But you're certainly not going to succeed by pacing like that. Now, I called Paula's parents. They're at Lake Tahoe, but they were going to pack their things and drive back immediately. Renee asked if I could stay with Paula until they got here. I canceled on Hank."

"I can stay with Paula," I said quickly.

"You need to solve this case," Mom insisted. "Paula didn't just fall. Petunia saw someone hit her over the head. It has to be related to the case. Go get Laurie, call Petunia for more details, and then sit down and do whatever brainstorming thing you do. You can do this. You're a natural."

"I don't know if I can, Mom," I whispered. "I keep coming up on dead ends, and now my best friend is hurt."

She knelt next to me and looked me in the eyes. "I've always been proud of you, my dear, but never more so since you had Laurie and took up this new, adventurous career."

Tears brimmed in my eyes.

She continued, "You're a great mom and a great investigator, and seeing you succeed has been the greatest privilege of my life. Don't tell your brother."

I laughed and wiped away the tears. "Okay. I'll go solve the case. As soon as the doctors let us know about Paula's scan results."

* * *

"KATE!" KENNY EXCLAIMED WHEN I WALKED INTO THE HOUSE. HE AND Laurie were sitting on the couch, reading a board book. "How's Paula?"

"She's going to be just fine," I said. "She has a concussion, but the imaging of her head looked pretty good, the doctor said."

"Oh, thank goodness."

Laurie reached for me, and I picked her up and gave her a big kiss.

"Thanks for coming on such short notice," I said. "How's Odette?"

A grin tugged on the corners of his mouth. "She's beautiful, as always."

I rolled my eyes and sighed dramatically, but then shot him a wink. "I hear you have a performance tonight?"

"Yup! For a one-night only musical with a full band. Odette's going to come see it."

"Nice!" I high-fived him with my free hand. From the look in his eyes, I knew I needed to add something else to my to-do list: *find a new babysitter*. I might not be comfortable with Kenny's relationship with Odette, but he was infatuated, and it didn't look like it was going away anytime soon.

He'd come through for me when I needed him, but I probably shouldn't count on him to be Mr. Reliable anymore.

"Just be careful, all right?" I said. "She's quite a bit older than you."

He rolled his eyes and sighed dramatically, imitating me. "Yes, Mom."

"Hey, now! I feed you meat pizza and all the cheese you want, and your mom only makes vegan food."

Shuddering, he said, "If I have to taste tofu one more time . . ."

"Get out of here." I waved him off. "You need to change and warm up. Get to your show early and work off some of the jitters."

I spent the early evening making a chart about the case. To anyone else, it would have looked like a huge mess—arrows pointing everywhere, lines drawn between persons of interest, six different colors of highlighter. But it helped me organize all the thoughts bouncing around in my head. But for one all-important question, I couldn't even dream up a reasonable theory

Why would someone attack Paula?

Maybe she'd seen something right before she was hit over the head, and she just couldn't remember?

Whiskers jumped in my lap, and I petted her absentmindedly.

But what could Paula have seen? Had some sort of evidence been left behind in the studio, something that neither the police nor any of the rest of us had been able to uncover? My head spun.

Sometimes cases got extra personal. Investigating my brother-in-law for murder had been personal. Going toe to toe with Jim's crazy ex-girlfriend had *definitely* been personal. And now this one had crossed that line. I'd wanted to solve the case to help save Dave's studio, but now the killer was coming after my best friend?

"You messed with the wrong private investigator, pal," I muttered under my breath.

A knock sounded at the door, and I jumped. But it was just Mom.

"Hey," I said, "Paula doing any better? Come in. I don't want Whiskers to get out."

"They discharged her," Mom said, coming inside.

Relief flooded me. "I'll call her!" I said, grabbing my phone.

"Let her rest," Mom said. "You can call her tomorrow. And here." Mom held out my black coat. "She asked me to bring this back to you. Something about high school and a polka-dotted sweater."

"Oh. Right. I'd already forgotten she had it," I murmured, reaching for the coat. "Thank you."

Then the scene flashed in my mind—Paula crumpled on the ground . . . wearing my black coat.

"The hood was up," I whispered. "She was wearing the hood."

Mom tilted her head in silent question.

The pieces clicked together, and it finally made sense.

My heart lurched and panic swelled in my chest. "They weren't targeting Paula," I blurted. "They mistook her for me."

A resigned look crossed Mom's face, and I realized she'd already figured that part out. "Be careful, dear," she said. "Should I stay here until Jim gets back?"

"The contractor is here, and I think that would dissuade anyone from trying something," I said, glancing out the window at the street. "But let me check when Jim is coming home."

Glancing at my texts, I realized I'd missed a couple of messages from Jim.

Invited Dave and bros over for dinner at seven. Forgot to tell you. Sorry.

My heart stopped. It was 6:17! I didn't have the time or bandwidth to plan and cook a meal for guests in less than forty-five minutes, much less clean the house. I had a case to solve!

But then I read Jim's next message. *Don't worry, I've got everything covered. Check the backyard.*

With a raised eyebrow, I showed the messages to Mom.

"Well, that's mysterious," she said. "Should we check it out?"

It was after sunset but before last light. I carried Laurie to the kitchen and peered out the window, looking for signs that anything was amiss. I couldn't see past the overgrown bushes in the planter beds, but it seemed like there was somehow a light on in the yard.

Odd. Then suspicion tightened my throat. What if the killer had somehow gotten to Jim? What if they'd stolen his phone and were trying to lure us into the backyard?

I texted Jim, *Tell me the name of your hermit crabs.*

As a child, Jim had moved around a lot, and his parents had used it as an excuse for why they couldn't have traditional pets like dogs or cats. To compensate, they'd bought him a series of much-loved hermit crabs, and Little Jim had called all the crabs by the same name.

Jim texted back almost immediately. *Captain Hook, why? I'm at the grocery store. Home in fifteen. Have you checked the backyard yet?*

Relief flooded me, and I motioned for Mom to follow me out onto the patio. When we went outside, my breath caught in my throat.

Our usually unkempt backyard lawn was mown, and a square pergola had been erected over our neglected outdoor table. The new structure smelled of fresh cedar. Two lines of elegant string lights ran from the corner of the house to the pergola, casting gentle yellow-white light, and more bulbs were draped beneath its eaves.

"When did you do this?" Mom cried.

"I . . . I don't know. This is the first time I've seen it." We drew closer to the pergola, and I realized that our outdoor table and its eight chairs had been re-stained and the grimy grill scrubbed until the stainless steel shone.

Jim really had taken care of everything. And, really, the timing of the dinner was perfect—chatting with Dave, Jack, and Eddie might actually help me make progress on the case.

In the fairy-tale lighting, Mom looked positively incandescent. "Jim did it as a surprise for you? Why, the sly fox. He didn't breathe a word about it to me."

Elbowing her, I said, "And you're already scheming to sneak back here with your boyfriends for romantic dates."

"Certainly you'll have to let me have a nice dinner here with Galigani. You can't keep this ambiance all to yourself, dear."

"I should probably at least clean the bathroom before the guys arrive," I said. "Could you play with Laurie while I give it a quick once-over?"

Ten minutes later, I declared the bathroom to be good enough. Mom pulled out of the driveway just as Jim drove up. I met him on the front porch. "Jim!" I cried. "It's beautiful! How did you pull it off?"

He climbed out of the car and started hauling in our groceries. "Jo-Jo already had the wood," he said, "and he gave us a great price on doing it as an add-on. I think he felt bad about the sewer incident. He put up the pergola and hung the lights, and I stained the furniture, scrubbed the grill, and mowed the lawn. I wanted it to be a surprise."

We went inside, and when he set the groceries on the counter, I stood on my tiptoes to plant a kiss on his cheek.

"You haven't even seen what I got yet!" He started unpacking the bags. "Steaks for the grill, Caesar salad in a bag, and pre-cooked mashed potatoes." With a deep bow, he added, "You're welcome."

I put the potatoes in the oven on the "keep warm" setting, and Jim seasoned the steaks.

"As soon as the guys get here," he said, "I'll fire up the grill!"

Dave and Eddie arrived right on time, Dave holding up a six-pack like it was a trophy as they walked into the backyard. Jim high-fived him and grabbed one of the beer cans.

"Oh, is it okay that I brought beer?" asked Dave, turning to me. "I just now remembered that you can't drink because of the babies."

"Go on ahead. Doesn't bother me a bit," I said from my seat at the outdoor table. Dave and Eddie joined me while Jim fired up the grill and started cooking the steaks.

"Hey, how's George?" Eddie called to Jim.

Jim glanced over at us with a wry expression on his face. His younger brother George was always a source of drama in our lives. "Hopefully getting into less trouble these days. He and his fiancée have a baby."

I really should call my soon-to-be sister-in-law, Kiku.

"Oh, do you like the fiancée?" asked Dave.

"Yeah," said Jim, "she's a nice girl. She's good for him."

Dave looked over at Laurie and held his arms out. "Wanna come see Uncle Dave?" he asked in a baby-talk voice.

She turned her face away from him and cuddled closer to me.

"Ha!" said Dave. "Someone's a mama's girl, huh?"

Kissing her head, I said, "I think she's been missing me. I've been running around even more than usual the last week or so."

"Thank you for that." Dave's face took on a serious cast. "Really. I don't think you know how much we appreciate your efforts."

"Speaking of my efforts, can we chat a little about the case?"

"Absolutely!" He took a slurp from his beer can. "Do you have any updates?"

"Nothing too concrete just yet, but I'm trying to double-check all the threads to see if I can find something that might point us in a tangible direction."

Jim joined us at the table. "Where's Jack?"

Eddie glanced at his phone. "Running late, I guess."

"That's not like him," said Jim, tapping his beer can.

"I'll call him." Eddie stood from the table and walked to the far side of the pergola while he dialed.

I asked a couple of questions about the dance teachers, and Eddie returned to the table shrugging.

"Oh!" Dave exclaimed, an exasperated expression on his face. "Did you see the paper today? They ran another piece about the murder and the fundraiser. We just can't get out from under the bad publicity."

"We should lean into it," Eddie argued, pressing his fingertips together. "Do something murder-mystery themed. We could announce it at the dance. Could we put together an escape room or something?"

Dave glared at Eddie. "Have some respect. A man is dead, and someone attacked Paula!"

Eddie raised his hands in this air. "I surrender, man. Sorry. That was in bad taste. We won't do it."

I asked a few more questions about the case, but Dave and Eddie didn't know any more than what they'd already told me.

That seemed to be a theme recently.

When Jim went to go pull the steaks off the grill, Dave asked, "Really, where is Jack? He's always on time."

"Makes me nervous," grunted Eddie. "With so many strange things going on . . . I'll call him again."

He dialed, and we fell silent. After a few moments, he shook his head. "No answer. Went straight to voicemail."

The atmosphere suddenly grew tense, but we tried to ignore it. I changed the subject, asking Dave how serious things were with Petunia.

"Pretty serious," he said with a grin. "If we get everything solved in time for the fundraiser and the event goes well, I'm going to propose to her at the end of the evening. I have the ring and everything."

I laughed aloud. "*Pretty serious* sounds like an understatement!"

Eddie's phone rang, and we jumped to attention. Surely this was Jack calling back, apologizing for being late, saying that something had come up and he'd be here soon.

But Eddie shook his head as he answered the phone. "I don't recognize the number." He accepted the call. "Hi, this is Eddie Goodrich . . . what? Jack, where are you? What?" His voice took on a frantic pitch.

Dave and I stared at each other. This didn't sound good.

"Okay," said Eddie. "Yeah, we'll be there right away."

His face was pale as he hung up. He looked from Dave to me. "That was Jack. He's . . . just been arrested for Leo's murder."

CHAPTER 15

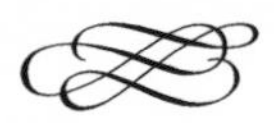

The guys piled into my car, since I was the only one who hadn't had anything to drink, and we sped to the police station.

"Take Laurie," I said to Jim as soon as we parked. "I want to see if I can find out what's going on from Deb."

Deb often worked in the afternoons and evenings—which I supposed worked best for her party-hard, sleep-off-the-hangovers lifestyle—but I didn't know for sure what her schedule was this week.

I led Dave and Eddie in and waved to the cop at the front desk. Though I didn't know him by name, he looked familiar, and I knew he'd recognize me. "I'm here to see Deb," I called. "They're with me."

He nodded and glanced back down at his computer screen without saying a word.

With a deep breath, I charged ahead toward Deb's office. The door was ajar. I peeked through the crack, and there she was, filling out paperwork.

Seemed like being a police officer was mostly paperwork.

"Knock, knock!" I called.

"Yo, Kate! Come on in," she said.

The three of us walked into her office, and she nodded at us. "Figured you'd come. I suppose you want the lowdown on the arrest in the dance studio case." She studied Dave and Eddie. "These the brothers?"

"Yes, ma'am," said Dave, his voice cracking.

She scoffed. "Don't *ma'am* me. This isn't Nashville. I'm Detective Fisher."

Oh, it was *Detective* Fisher now? That explained why she'd been at the crime scene with McNearny.

She shot me a grin. "Told you we need a girls' night. I've got a lot of news to catch you up on." Then she glanced at Dave and Eddie again, and her face took on a more serious, professional cast. "Can you guys step outside so I can speak freely with Kate?"

Dave turned desperate eyes on me.

"It's okay," I said, setting a reassuring hand on his arm. "I'll fight for him. There's some kind of mistake. I'm sure of it. Go back down to the lobby and find Jim."

Dave and Eddie hesitated, looking at each other, then withdrew from Deb's office.

"Shut the door behind you," Deb called. The door thudded closed. "Sit down."

I took a seat opposite her. "Tell me exactly what's going on. Jack's been arrested?"

She grimaced. "Not formally. For now, he's being detained while we question him."

I bolted to my feet. "Is he being questioned right now?"

"He's sitting in the interrogation room, waiting. McNearny is giving him plenty of time to think about his life choices."

"What's the case against him?" I asked. "I can't imagine . . ."

"You should have a better imagination." Deb leaned forward over the desk. "People are capable of a lot worse than we think."

"No," I said firmly. "We've known the brothers forever. They're Jim's best friends."

Deb nodded. "We found some of Jack's DNA on Leo. Hair on Leo's shirt. We were able to pull DNA samples for people affiliated with the studio off of cups, and Jack's turned out to be the match."

"They worked together," I said. "There are a lot of reasons Jack's hair could be on the shirt."

Deb shrugged. "It's more solid than any of the other theories we have."

"Has Jack called an attorney?"

"He didn't seem to know who to call. That's why he called his brother."

I stood abruptly and walked to the door. "I know I owe you ten thousand favors already, but please do what you can to stall McNearny."

"You know I'll do it if you want me to," said Deb. "But don't let feelings cloud your judgment. Just because you know and like the guy doesn't mean he's not guilty. Everyone's shocked when someone they know turns out to be a killer."

"And you know I'll follow the evidence where it leads," I replied. "That I've no intention of letting anyone get away with murder."

"I know." She leaned back and laced her fingers behind her head. "That's why I'll stall for you."

"Thank you." I bolted back to the lobby, where Jim and Eddie were conferring in low tones and Dave was talking on the phone.

"Who's he on the line with?" I asked, gesturing toward Dave.

"A lawyer." Eddie's hands were balled into fists. "We looked up some local ones with good reviews. I think he called Neil Taylor."

I snatched the phone out of Dave's hand and hung up. Dave looked at me incredulously. I tossed the phone back to him. "You're not going to hire Neil Taylor."

"Is he not any good?" Dave asked.

I'd already pulled open the contacts app on my phone. "I haven't heard of him," I said. "I'm calling in a favor." I hit *dial*.

After a few seconds, a familiar voice greeted me.

"Barramendi," I said. "I need you to drop what you're doing and meet me at the precinct."

* * *

Gary Barramendi, the highest-profile criminal defense attorney on the West Coast, strolled into station looking totally unphased. "Kate," he said, reaching out and shaking my hand, his thin, six-foot-six frame towering over all of us. "A pleasure, as always."

I briefly explained the situation. "Can you get him out of here for us?"

Barramendi's already-asymmetrical face contorted into a look of wry amusement. "Can I get him out of here?" he scoffed. He practically stalked over to the cop at the desk. "I'm here to speak with my client."

The cop looked slightly annoyed—this was not the precinct's first run-in with Gary the Grizzly—but waved him back.

Eddie looked at me with an awed expression. "That guy's on TV all the time. You know him?"

"We've done some work together. And last month I took down the guy who tried to murder his cousin. And that's why you're not going to hire Neil Taylor," I said, taking a bow.

But I forgot to account for the weight of my pregnant belly and pitched forward, grabbing onto a chair to steady myself. I regained my feet with an expression of calm serenity, daring any of the guys to acknowledge my fall. "Has anyone called Sharon?" I asked, taking a seat next to Jim and Laurie.

"She's visiting her mom in Oregon," Dave replied, his leg bouncing. "I didn't want to worry her."

"She should know," I said gently.

We waited in tense silence, and I turned Deb's words over in my head. *People are capable of a lot worse than we think. Everyone's shocked when someone they know turns out to be a killer.*

Jack had always been good friends with Jim's younger brother George. They horsed around together as teens and young adults and were always causing trouble. But murder? There was absolutely no way.

And anyway, what possible motive could Jack have? Whoever had killed Leo was trying to sabotage the studio and the fundraiser that was being held for Jack's benefit. Could stopping the fundraiser have been his motive? Maybe killing Leo had been an accident.

Was it possible that Jack didn't want children? Was he thinking of leaving Sharon?

None of that made sense, though. If he was going to leave Sharon, he could do it whether or not we threw a fundraiser for them. I knew Jack, he'd just call off the fundraiser, not stage some elaborate hoax to ruin things.

People are capable of a lot worse than we think.

What about Hank? My breath caught in my throat. Hank was at the studio today when Paula was hurt! He could have hit her over the head, thinking it was me. He knew we were investigating him. He was an investor in Monte's studio.

What if his reappearance in Mom's life wasn't a coincidence? What if he was trying to get close to me to throw me off the scent?

We'd run into Hank before Leo's death. But the strange events at the studio had been happening for weeks. Had he found out we were helping with the fundraiser and tracked us down on purpose? Pretended it was a chance meeting?

I texted Galigani, *Might have a motive for Hank.*

My phone rang immediately, and I excused myself and went into the parking lot to take the call.

"Hey, Galigani." As quietly as I could, I explained what Petunia had said about Hank being a supporter of the arts and what I'd seen on Monte's computer.

Galigani let out a low whistle. "Good work, kid."

"By the way, what was this thing about you telling Mom that you didn't want anything serious?"

He hemmed and hawed. "I do want something serious with her. But maybe the engagement ring thing was a little premature. I think I started realizing that when Hank came back in the picture."

"Do you really think it's premature?" I asked, sitting on a concrete bench. "Or is this sour grapes because you don't think *she* wants anything serious?"

"You heard Hank," he grumped. "She loves me. Sure, she's since decided to go out on a date or two with him, but he's not going to win her over. Your mother and I have got a good thing going, and there's no reason to put that kind of pressure on it yet."

"Do you mean that?"

I could hear his gulp through the phone line.

"I just want her to choose me from a place of full freedom," he said softly. "And be certain of her decision. I don't want her to look back and resent me for pushing her too quickly. I've been letting jealousy run my decisions, and I know it's not a good look."

"If you say so," I said with a sigh. "Can you start looking into Hank right away? Like, tonight? I'm at the police station springing Dave's little brother."

"The brother? Which one?"

"Jack."

"What?" Galigani barked. "Isn't he the one who was going to benefit from the fundraiser in the first place?"

"Apparently some of his hairs were on Leo's shirt."

"Hmm," said Galigani. "That's not great, but it's not damning, either. We'll need a good explanation for it."

"I brought in Barramendi to get him out."

"Well done." He chuckled, and pride swelled in his voice.

The door to the station swung open, and Barramendi strode out, followed by a small entourage: Dave and Eddie, Jim and Laurie . . . and last of all, Jack.

My heart leaped into my throat. "I've gotta go," I said into the phone. "Check into that lead for me, and let's talk tomorrow. Thank you. I appreciate it. I really do."

I hung up and looked expectantly at Barramendi.

"The cops have nothing," said Barramendi confidently. "Leo borrowed Jack's shirt after he spilled coffee on himself that morning. His shirt was stained, and Jack had an extra one in the dressing room. We can prove it, too, because Jack gets all his shirts altered. Plus, Jack remembers seeing Leo stuff the coffee-stained shirt in his cubby, and I have it on good authority from your friend Debbie—"

"Deb," I interjected.

"Right, Deb. I have it on good authority from her that they did, in fact, recover a coffee-stained shirt from Leo's cubby. If they file charges, we'll trounce them in court."

Jack looked shell-shocked, and Dave slung a comforting arm around his shoulder.

"Do you think they'll file charges?" asked Eddie quietly, looking worried. "Even if we win, the expense of going to trial . . ."

Barramendi quirked his mouth. "Hard to say what they'll try to make stick. It's not a strong case, but there's a possibility they'll file charges if they can't find any other suspect. And the way the press has been following the case..." Barramendi let out a low whistle. "Did you see the article about McNearny *pussyfooting* around the case? They went to town with all the dancing puns and the photo of him? Worst photo in the world." Barramendi's face contorted and I could see he was holding in a laugh.

"It's not funny!" I said, poking Barramendi in the ribs, and simultaneously holding in my own laugh.

Although I hadn't seen the article, making McNearny mad could never work in my favor.

Barramendi smiled. "Don't worry—I owe you Kate, and I'm not going to let this get unjustly pinned on your friend."

I nodded. "Thank you."

"It's never easy," Barremendi said, compassion returning to his face. "And we know the best defense is a good offense. Do you want to me see if Vicente can help on the PI side? He's still recovering, but I know he's itching to get back to work."

I gritted my teeth. I hating coming up empty, and I wanted nothing less than the Vicente Domingo shoeing in on my case and possibly solving it before me. But, for Jack and Sharon's sake, I set aside my pride and said, "I won't say no to more help."

Because at the end of the day, this wasn't about me. This was about justice, about clearing Jack's name . . . and most of all, about catching the killer before they struck again.

CHAPTER 16

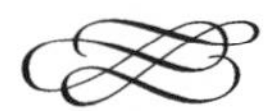

Jo-Jo's power tools were at it again at the crack of dawn two mornings later, like a robotic rooster determined to wake the world, but when I thought of the beautiful new pergola in the backyard, I minded the noise less.

Somehow Laurie was sleeping through it, so I took the opportunity to open the boxes of babyproofing gadgets and inspect the cabinets. The latches came with little screws to hold them in place, and it looked like the previous owners of the house had drilled tiny holes for babyproofing locks in the cabinets already. I squinted from the locks to the cabinet doors. I was pretty sure I could do this myself with a screwdriver.

The only problem was that I wasn't sure where our toolbox was. I checked the laundry room, under the kitchen sink, in the bathroom. Nowhere. Ordinarily, Jim kept the toolbox in the garage, but I knew he'd brought it in the house before Jo-Jo started work—we'd cleared every last thing out of the garage.

I went into the bedroom and tried to rouse Jim. "Hey, honey," I called.

No answer.

I inspected him more closely and realized he'd put in earplugs to drown out the construction noise. With a sigh, I shook his shoulder.

"Yeah?" he said groggily.

"Where is the toolbox?" I practically yelled.

"Sounds good, honey," he replied before turning over and going back to sleep.

I let out an exasperated sigh.

After stopping to think, I went back out into the living room and eyed the door to the garage. I didn't know where Jim had put our toolbox, but Jo-Jo certainly had a sea of screwdrivers.

Yes, I decided. Laurie was getting better and better at grabbing things. I wanted to get the locks installed as soon as possible, and this was a rare free moment when I couldn't follow up on anything case-related—no doubt most everyone else was fast asleep.

Except our contractor and his power tools, apparently.

I went into the garage and saw Jo-Jo and another redheaded man. Jo-Jo was working with a drill, and the other man seemed to be doing something with the electrical wiring. Jo-Jo saw me and waved, setting down the drill. The garage fell mercifully silent.

"Morning, lassie," called Jo-Jo. "This is me cousin, Liam. He's doing the electric for ya."

I waved at Liam. "Thank you. It's looking great!" Really, it looked like a mess of dust and wiring, but surely by the time all the work was done, this mess would somehow be the perfect nursery for the twins.

I hoped.

"Sorry, about this," I said, shifting my weight from foot to foot, "but I was wondering if I could borrow a screwdriver." I held up the package of babyproofing locks. "I'm trying to make the house safe for Laurie. She's starting to get into things."

"Ah, of course, that's grand," said Jo-Jo, running over to a work-bench and rummaging through a toolbox. "Let me see the screws . . . ah, this one should do the trick."

I thanked him and went back inside, feeling jubilant at the thought of taking the project into my own hands.

Rosie the Riveter, reporting for duty.

I'd gotten about half of the locks done when Galigani called, "Hey, kid, I found something. Looks like a real break in the case."

Excitement jolted up my spine. "Tell me."

Laurie started fussing, so I set the screwdriver on the kitchen counter and went to pick her up, clutching the phone between my ear and shoulder.

"I checked out the books at *Tre Fratelli Danzanti*," Galigani said. "And something really interesting stood out to me about Hank."

"Yes?"

"The picture you sent me from Monte's showed that Hank invested in Dare to Dance right after *Tre Fratelli Danzanti* finished repaying his loan."

I tried to interpret what it meant. It was suspicious, certainly. What had caused Hank to have this change of heart? Why had he switched allegiances? Was it just a business opportunity that had presented itself?

Was he now trying to help Monte take over the brothers' studio altogether?

"Anyway, I'll have a little chat with Hank today," said Galigani. "Want to come along?"

"Definitely," I said. "But let me touch base with Paula to see how she's doing and if she needs anything from me."

I called Paula next. "How are you feeling, girl?"

"I'm better. Still have a terrible headache," Paula said.

"Well, you took a pretty big blow to the head. Scared the daylights out of me," I said.

"YEAH. THANK YOU FOR CARING!" SHE SAID.

I laughed. "Like I could help it. I swear if anything happens to you….I'll…well…I don't know what I'll do, but we're supposed to grow old together so don't ruin my plans."

She chuckled. "I'm doing my best to stay alive. Speaking of which, I think Petunia might kill me if I don't get the decorations up before the event. Can you come to the studio today to help me?"

"Of course, but are you sure you should be working?" I asked in concern.

"The doctors told me I had to lie around and do nothing strenuous

—but I think if I can just boss you around it won't be strenuous for me at all."

"Ha! Okay, count me in."

Even though I wanted to investigate Hank, I knew Galigani could take care of that without me. My best friend needed my help—someone had to make sure she didn't overwork herself. Plus, helping Paula would give me a chance to hang out around the studio and watch for anything suspicious. Maybe she'd even remember something about the moment she was knocked out.

I texted Galigani to let him know I was going to the studio instead. Then I got Laurie ready for the day. I put her in a cute little floral dress and added a flower headband. "If you'll leave that on for just a little bit," I said in a high-pitched voice, "I'll be able to show everyone how you match Miss Petunia!"

She tugged it off her head with a gurgle of glee.

"Little duck!" I exclaimed, putting it back on. She wiggled and batted at it, dislodging it.

Laurie had quite the mind of her own, and I knew there was no way I was going to win this battle. So, I abandoned the floral headband and added a tiny pink sweater to the ensemble.

It took twice as long to get ready as seemed reasonable, but finally we headed out the door. We parked, and I sat without moving for a moment, staring at the storefront of *Tre Fratelli Danzanti*. "Three days," I whispered. "We only have three more days to figure this out."

I bundled Laurie into the stroller, and as we headed into the studio, I spotted my mom's car several spots down. "Grandma's here!" I said to Laurie.

Sure enough, another ghastly-looking concoction was perched on the front desk when we walked in. It appeared to be some sort of layered gelatin salad—or perhaps a monster from Candy Land. The dish was about half empty, so it couldn't taste too bad. Mom's recipes really all had turned out fairly tasty. But . . . we couldn't present this to the event attendees. It just didn't look appetizing.

Good luck explaining that to mom.

I headed back toward the sound of voices and found Mom and Paula hanging decorations in the first partitioned-off classroom.

Further down, I could hear music. No doubt there was a lesson of some kind going on.

"Darling!" Mom called when she saw me.

Paula whirled, her hands full of black-and-white checkered fabric. "Oh, I'm so glad you're here. I have a pounding headache, but we have to get this part done today." She held up the cloth to emphasize her point.

"We will get done whatever you need to get done," I said in a calming voice. "Just show me what to do."

She showed me how to drape and hang the fabric, and I got to work up on a footstool, setting Laurie on the ground next to me. "So, Mom," I said, "what was up with that dessert out front?"

Mom, who had just finished draping the last of the cloth she was holding, clapped her hands in glee and scooped Laurie off the ground. "Why, it's a seven-layer gelatin salad, dear."

Paula looked a little green and whispered, "I didn't try it."

Mom pursed her lips. "Well, everyone who *did* try it liked it. Why, it's mostly eaten already."

I hung another strip of fabric. "Maybe we should try to come up with something that looks a little more appetizing? It doesn't matter how good it is if it doesn't fit the aesthetic."

"I tried to tell her," murmured Paula.

Affronted, Mom said, "These are genuine 1950s recipes. I got them out of my mother's cookbook."

"I'm sure they are," I said in a soothing tone, "and they've all tasted great. Grandma was a wonderful cook, but the guests at the event aren't going to know that. They're going to make all their decisions based on what they can see, and you won't have the opportunity to persuade them to give the iffy-looking food a chance."

Mom seemed to consider this, and then nodded, appeased. "Well, I'll go look at all the recipes again when I'm home, and work on figuring out what will look the best. Perhaps that's even more important than how it tastes."

"Maybe split the difference 50/50," I offered. If she focused *only* on what it looked like . . . I shuddered as I imagined what some of the recipes might end up being. "Make sure that it looks great but also tastes pretty good."

"Of course," she said, and her face was already alight with possibilities. "Oh, there are one or two I remember that I think will be just perfect."

"No savory popsicles," I warned as I moved the footstool down a few feet.

"But what if—"

"No savory popsicles," said Paula and I in unison.

Out of the corner of my eye, I saw Odette stride down the hall, past the door to the room we were decorating. Kenny wasn't with her.

"Hey, Odette," I called.

She stopped, glared at me, and stalked onward.

Paula and I shared a look. "What was that about?" I asked. "Did I make her mad, or something?"

"Maybe she just woke up grumpy," said Paula.

"Give me a second. I want to see what's going on. Just in case I can dig up anything relevant."

I followed Odette down the hall and found her in one of the classrooms.

"What's up?" I called.

She spun around, rage contorting her features. I took a step back. I'd never seen this side of her.

"Kenny stood me up two nights ago," she spat. "Because he was *babysitting* for you."

I held up my hands in a conciliatory gesture. "Hey, I'm sorry. It was an emergency."

Odette rolled her eyes. "Get out."

My temper flared, and I fought to keep myself calm. "Now, listen here. Kenny's left me in a bind over and over again the past couple of weeks because he's been spending every waking moment with you. And now you're mad because one time—*one time*—when we had an actual emergency when my best friend was in the hospital, he skipped out on your date?" I practically yelled the word *date*.

Guess I hadn't kept myself calm.

But the audacity! How was *Kenny* the one just out of high school?

Did this girl—this grown woman, for crying out loud—think the whole world revolved around her? How self-absorbed could she be? Did she insist that her boyfriends only ever consider her feelings and never anyone else's? I'd been concerned about Odette and Kenny as a couple for a while, but now I was certain. Kenny needed to ditch her for good.

How am I going to convince him?

"Well," said Odette, her voice deadly quiet, "he'll be reliable for you now. I quit the music video. I'm not going to see him again."

Then again, maybe I wouldn't have to talk him out of it. But she was quitting the music video over her hurt feelings? After all the work Kenny had put into it? Could she be any more selfish?

Crossing my arms, I said, "Kenny spent a lot of time setting that up. You're just walking out midway through, before it's done?"

Odette shrugged. "I guess so," she said flippantly. "Now, get out. I have a class to teach."

CHAPTER 17

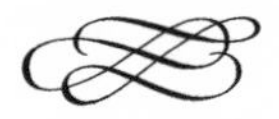

When I got home that evening, I called Kenny. For the first time in weeks, he picked up on the first ring. "Kate?" His voice sounded dry and cracked, and my heart broke for him.

"I ran into Odette at the studio," I said gently. "She told me about what happened."

"She did? How did she seem?"

I hesitated. "Angry."

He gave a long, desperate sigh.

"Want to come over? I'll order an all-meat pizza."

He laughed, and I thought I detected a hint of the old Kenny somewhere beneath his angst. No doubt layers of pepperoni, Italian sausage, and ham would start to bring him back to the land of the living.

A knock sounded on the door, and Kenny said, "I'm already here."

Chuckling, I said, "It's unlocked. Come on in."

Kenny pushed open the door, and Laurie immediately reached for him. I dialed our favorite pizza place and placed an order for an extra-large all-meat pizza with extra meat.

"Can you get wings too?" he asked.

I rolled my eyes. "Do you think your metabolism is normal?"

He looked confused.

"Anything else?" I asked. "There's a coupon for a free pizza-size chocolate chip cookie."

He shook his head and sank onto the couch, still holding Laurie.

I finished placing the order, adding the cookie on for myself. My metabolism may not be as fast as his, but I had little beings to nurture and I was fairly certain they were partial to chocolate.

I sat down on the couch next to Kenny. He sighed.

Poor kid is absolutely crushed.

After a long pause, he said, "I think I have enough footage to finish editing the music video."

"Good!" I exclaimed. "I know you put a lot of work into that."

He fidgeted. "I just don't know if I have the heart to finish. All that footage of Odette and me dancing . . ."

"You should finish it. It's a cool concept. But it's all right to set it aside for a bit while everything is still fresh."

He sighed. "I was going to enter it into a contest. Entries are due at the end of the month."

"I'm sorry," I said after a long pause. "I feel responsible—"

"It's not your fault. I needed to help out. It was important. She just . . . can't seem to see that. Maybe it's for the best." He abruptly changed the subject. "Miss Laurie is getting so big!"

We played with Laurie until the pizza arrived, and Kenny brightened at the sight of the all-meat pizza with extra meat and the heaping pile of wings.

"Stuff yourself to the brim," I ordered. "Best cure for a broken heart."

At the scent of food, Whiskers immediately materialized from wherever she'd been hiding. She rubbed up against me, pleading for a bite.

"Little scammer," I said. But I pulled a piece of ham off my slice of pizza and fed her from my hand.

Kenny gorged himself on the pizza, folding the slices in half and stuffing them into this mouth at an alarming rate.

"Don't choke," I said.

He chuckled and said through a mouth-full, "Don't worry. I'm a professional."

I smiled, relief setting over me.

Kenny and Odette have broken up!

I had my babysitter back, at least until Kenny went off to college. Selfish to even think in those terms, I knew, but it was so clear that Odette wasn't good for him.

Yes, it was painful for him to have the band-aid ripped off, but this was the best outcome for everyone.

Whiskers clambered onto my lap and reared up, trying to take a bite directly out of the pizza.

"No," I said scowling. "This is not your pizza."

I ate one slice of the pizza—minus a few pieces of meat that I fed to Whiskers—and two wings, and Kenny devoured the rest of the food. He collapsed backward on the ground, a satisfied smile on his face. "You're right. The broken heart hurts a little less, I think. I might need you to order me a meat pizza every night this month."

"Don't count on it," I said with a smirk.

"Is there ice cream?" he asked.

I laughed. "Of course! In the freezer. I was planning to pile it on top of that pizza-sized cookie."

Kenny scrambled to his feet. "I'm going to beat you to it!" Suddenly, his phone rang, and his eyes widened when he glanced at the screen.

Oh no . . .

He answered the phone, his voice squeaking, "Odette?"

I rubbed my temples and let out a sigh.

Kenny shuffled his feet. "Yes. Please. Absolutely. I'll be there in ten minutes." He ran to the door as he hung up. "Sorry, Kate. Thanks for the food! I think I might be able to patch things up with Odette. Maybe I won't need all those pizzas after all!"

The door closed behind him before I could blink.

Laurie stared mournfully after Kenny and let out a sad whimper.

"Oh, little duck. He'll be back. Eventually. That relationship is definitely not going to last." I picked her up and planted kisses on her cheek.

Well, so much for that taking care of itself.

Galigani called soon after. "I talked to Hank," he said.

"Oh?" Anticipation and dread warred in my chest. I didn't want it to be Hank. But if it wasn't Hank, who could it be?

Not Jack. Anyone but Jack.

Well, anyone but Jack or Sharon or Eddie or Dave or Petunia.

Galigani sounded altogether disappointed when he said, "I really don't think it's Hank. Turns out that his niece started working as a teacher at Dare to Dance, and he was giving them money to make sure they stayed open. He quit giving them money and announced he wanted to sell his share in the company—and the niece quit her job—when they learned from your mom about the plan to poach *Tre Fratelli Danzanti's* students. Said it's not how honest people did business. He showed me the emails he sent, and I talked to the niece too."

Laurie grabbed at the phone, and I set her down on the ground next to the newly babyproofed cabinets.

"When did he send the emails?" I asked, tossing the pizza box in the kitchen trash. "Was it after we questioned him? Could he be trying to throw us off his trail?"

"Well, of course it was. We didn't know what was going on with Todd and Kim until after that. But . . . he also showed me his investment accounts and bank records."

I wrinkled my nose. "His investment accounts?"

The front door opened and closed, and Jim came into the kitchen and gave me a kiss. I pointed to the phone and mouthed, *Galigani*. Jim nodded, picked up Laurie, and carried her into the living room.

"Suffice it to say Petunia wasn't kidding when she said he was loaded. His pharmacy business has always made good money, and he turned it into a fortune in the stock market. He bought a load of Amazon stock at twenty bucks a share. Made some other good stock picks too. Let's just say this guy doesn't care if he loses twenty grand. Certainly not worth killing anyone over."

I whistled. "Imagine being so rich you don't care if you lose twenty grand."

"Oh, I've been imagining it half the day, kid." Undeniable jealousy laced Galigani's voice.

"And he's still working as a pharmacist?"

"He says it keeps him busy but that he's glad the business runs itself so he can travel as much as he wants. Hey, kid?"

"Yeah?"

"Don't tell your mom how rich Hank is. He says he doesn't really tell anyone, but that he figured he'd make an exception to clear his name so that we could spend our energy chasing the real killer."

"You worried his money will make him impossibly attractive?" I teased.

"That much money never hurt a man's chances," he grumped. "Besides, he doesn't want her to know. Wants her to make her choice without being influenced by all that, and I can't say I blame him."

"My lips are sealed." I grabbed a washcloth and started wiping down the counter. "I suppose that means the gambling debt theory is a dead end, too."

"If Hank had anything to do with Leo's death, it was personal, not business," said Galigani. "And we've got no reason to think he had anything personal against him."

Leaning over the counter, I sighed. "Then what on earth is going on?"

"I don't know," said Galigani grimly. "But we're running out of time to figure it out."

We hung up, and I set the rag in the sink and stared morosely at my to-do list, letting my thoughts run unimpeded.

To Do:

1. ~~Talk with Galigani re: Hank.~~
2. Check in with Paula.
3. Find Wonder Woman thing for Nick's wife? What do nerds like?
4. ~~Finish babyproofing every cabinet Laurie can reach.~~
5. ~~Hang posters around town.~~
6. Get new prime suspect.
7. Figure out childcare.

I'D CHECKED OFF NEARLY HALF THE ITEMS, BUT *GET A NEW PRIME SUSPECT* sent shivers of anxiety down my spine. It wasn't just that I needed a new prime suspect—with only three days left until the fundraiser, I needed to catch a killer before someone else got hurt.

And I desperately needed reliable childcare.

Jim walked into the room and frowned. "You okay? You look worried."

"I think we need to find another nanny," I said, sitting cross-legged on the floor.

Jim's brows furrowed. "Is Kenny not working out? I know he's been wrapped up in his new girlfriend, but the infatuation phase will pass soon." Jim scooped Laurie into the air and she giggled.

"It's not just that. I don't think that relationship is going to last. And I'm not saying we need to replace him altogether," I said.

Jim plopped Laurie on to the little rocking horse Hank had given her, and she squealed in delight.

Whiskers scooted out from beneath the couch and jumped into my lap. I petted her impossibly soft fur.

"But I need to have reliable childcare if I'm going to do this job. Part of me feels like I'd be further along in the case if I'd been able to follow leads immediately instead of worrying about who was going to watch Laurie. And once the twins get here? There's no way I can haul two infants and a toddler around."

"No," Jim said absently. "It's not safe. I don't want you to have to worry about that. Do I smell pizza?"

"Kenny ate it all," I said.

Jim made a face. "That kid. Where does he put all? Do you think his legs are hollow?"

"They have to be," I said.

"Let's keep Kenny as our evening babysitter," Jim said. "But I think you need someone more regular to watch Laurie during the day when we're both trying to work."

I bit my lip. "Do you think we can afford that?"

"Not if you keep taking cases pro bono for friends," Jim said with a laugh. "But yes, with the contracts I've signed with clients for the next six months, I think we could arrange for a nanny if you get paid for your cases."

Laurie clapped and let out a yell, but Jim's steady hand kept her in the saddle. I caressed my baby bump. How I loved our little family. And how I loved that I had a career that excited me and that still allowed me more time with my baby than my old office manager job ever would have given me.

"Somehow we'll make it work," I murmured.

Jim reached out with his free hand and threaded his fingers through mine. "Should we put out an ad for a nanny?" His mouth quirked like he'd tasted something way too salty.

"You hate that idea as much as I do, huh?"

He laughed aloud. "Great minds think alike. Why don't I ask for referrals from a couple of colleagues whose little ones just started preschool? No doubt they'll know of some good nannies."

I jumped at the idea. "And I'll talk to Paula. She's been networking in a lot of female entrepreneur circles. I bet she knows people who can point us to good babysitters too. We can run an ad if we exhaust our options, but I'd rather not do that unless we're desperate."

"Agreed," said Jim.

* * *

TWO MORNINGS LATER, I TEXTED PAULA TO CHECK ON HER. SHE REPLIED that her head was still fuzzy and that she was having a slow morning. So, I bundled Laurie into the car, saying, "Let's go see Auntie Paula!"

When we arrived, I checked Paula's pupils and asked her a couple questions, to make sure she wasn't having concussion complications, and then I set Laurie down on the floor near baby Chloe while I played superhero action figures with two-year-old Danny.

"How's the case coming?" Paula asked.

I groaned. "Don't remind me. I spent all day yesterday chasing leads and got absolutely nowhere."

"I'm sorry."

"Me too."

After a long pause, she rubbed her temples and grimaced. "Can you keep an eye on everyone for a few minutes so I can hop in the shower? I'm hoping the hot water will ease my headache."

"Of course!"

"You're a lifesaver!" she called as she disappeared into the master bedroom.

Fifteen minutes later, she emerged with damp hair and a serene expression. "My head still hurts, but that helped a lot."

While Paula nursed Chloe and kept an eye on Laurie, I made breakfast for Danny—nutrition-packed waffles and a cup of halved grapes.

"Hey, do any of your fancy professional friends know of good nannies?" I called from the kitchen. "I think we need to hire a day nanny so that I always have childcare when I'm working on a case."

"Yikes," said Paula, "Kenny's shoes are tough to fill. I can definitely get you some names, but I don't know if they'll be as good as Kenny."

I loaded the breakfast onto Danny's highchair and then tugged it to the edge of the kitchen so that I could see Paula while supervising Danny. With a grunt, I swung him up into the chair. I was used to an eight-month-old, Danny felt *so* heavy.

He bit straight into the waffle but knocked the grapes all over the floor. "No! Skin!" he yelled.

I stared at Paula. "He wants grapes without skins?"

She shrugged, an exasperated look on her face. "Apparently."

As much as I adored Danny, there was no way I was going to individually peel grapes. We compromised on a banana.

"Look, no skin!" I said as I handed him slices.

He grunted at me but was mollified enough to eat the banana. Meanwhile, Paula and I chitchatted as she finished feeding Chloe, and when everyone had eaten enough breakfast, we got the kids ready for the day.

"I'm taking the kids to my mom's place," said Paula. "Do you want to see if she'll watch Laurie, too?"

"That'd be great! Laurie loves your mom."

"And then I'm going to put the finishing touches on the decorating. Would you mind running by the studio just to look at everything and make sure I'm not missing anything big? It's always helpful to get an extra set of eyes, and with this head injury, I don't trust my own judgment. It's okay if you don't have time . . ."

"Of course! I *always* have time for you. Plus, I've done nothing but run into walls while focusing on the case recently. Sometimes my best breakthroughs come when I let myself focus on other things for a little while. Maybe my subconscious will figure something out while I'm looking at the decor."

Paula's mom agreed to watch Laurie, so Paula took all the kids in her car, and I headed off to the studio to inspect Paula's handiwork.

When I walked into the first partitioned-off room, I let out a little gasp. As always, Paula had outdone herself. Each room was decorated in a classy mix of black-and-white and pale pink. Silhouettes of swing dancers hung from the walls, and bouquets of balloons waited to be placed on tables. An authentic-looking jukebox and three food tables that looked like diner counters complete with barstools finished off the festive atmosphere. It was elegant and beautiful—the perfect blend of kitschy theme night and sophisticated ambiance.

"Looks great, doesn't it?" Dave asked from behind me.

I turned to face him. "Paula always comes through." I glanced down at the dance floor. "I just hope I come through."

Dave put his arm out and spun me around the room. Dancing with him was always a thrill. He stopped abruptly with me mid dip, his strong arm around my waist. "Do you trust me not to you let you drop, Kate?"

"Without a doubt. I trust you completely," I said.

"As I do you. I have faith in you," he said. "We all do."

He righted me and I smiled.

"I'm back at square one," I confessed. "I don't know if there's any way to crack the case in time. What if there's another death and I could have prevented it?"

"Well, doll," called an altogether-too-smooth and altogether-too-familiar voice. "Maybe I can help you out with that."

I looked at the newcomer holding a motorcycle helmet in the doorway. "Hey, Vicente."

CHAPTER 18

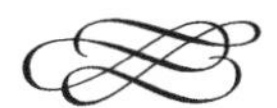

"Gary asked me to poke around," said Vicente by way of explanation. As usual, he was dressed in all black, looking entirely too sexy for his own good. "He said you might need a little help on a case for one of his clients. And I've got something for you."

"Shouldn't you be resting?" I asked, crossing my arms.

A devious grin crossed his face. "Resting? I've been out of the hospital for a month! How long do you think a bullet is supposed to keep me down?"

I chuckled and introduced Vicente and Dave and then ushered Vicente out of the studio. "Tell me about your lead," I said as soon as we reached the parking lot.

Vicente pressed his fingertips together. "How much have you looked into Hank Henning?"

Slumping back against the building dramatically, I said, "*That's* what you have for me? We've cleared Hank. He has no motive."

"I think he does," retorted Vicente.

"And that"—I crossed my arms—"is why I don't need your help to solve this case. Let me guess. You found out that Hank invested money in Dare to Dance and think he wanted to help Monte run *Tre Fratelli Danzanti* into the ground so he could recoup his investment."

"And *that,*" Vicente said with a bow, "is why I'll always be a step ahead of you on the investigations, doll."

"You know, I'd like you better if you dropped the chauvinism."

He continued, unruffled, "What if I told you that Leo and Hank patronized the same underground poker ring, and Leo owed Hank money?"

"Galigani looked into the poker angle. It doesn't make any sense. It's a poker night, not an *underground poker ring,* and the stakes were never that high. Plus, what's someone as rich as Hank doing risking going to jail over poker money when he already has more money than he could spend in a lifetime?"

"Wasn't about the money," said Vicente, swinging his motorcycle helmet up onto his head. "Not really. It was personal. Hank didn't need the money, but he was enraged about being stiffed. The principle of the thing, you know. Two witnesses at poker saw him threaten Leo."

"They didn't tell Galigani that."

Vicente scoffed. "Galigani smells like a cop. They're not going to tell him anything that brings police sniffing around their operation."

"You, on the other hand," I said lightly, "have the air of someone who just wants to show up to poker and have all his money taken away from him."

He grinned and strode to his motorcycle, several parking spaces down. "You know, I was a card shark in Vegas for a few months," he called.

"Of course you were," I muttered. Then, more loudly, I asked, "Then why go to all the trouble of sabotaging the studio?"

Vicente revved up the motorcycle. Rolling my eyes, I walked closer so I could hear him.

"Hank didn't sabotage the studio," he said. "He heard about the strange goings-on from Leo at poker night and decided it was his opportunity. He could get revenge on Leo without getting caught because everyone would be focused on the sabotage element and wouldn't look as closely at Leo's enemies."

With that, he gave me a satisfied nod and drove off. I stood on the sidewalk in shock. So, if Vicente was right, nothing was really going to happen at the fundraiser. The note was just a distraction technique.

I turned it over in my head, considering all the angles.

But the theory wasn't sitting right with me. Could Galigani have been so completely wrong about poker night? And was Hank really the kind of guy to scheme murder over being affronted? I'd have to look more into the poker thing if Mom kept dating Hank—if he had threatened someone over poker debt, I didn't want her anywhere near him.

But was he really the killer?

Something just didn't fit.

I wandered back into the studio, turning the idea over in my head. "Hey, Dave!" I called.

"Yeah?" He poked his head out of the office at the end of the hall.

"Question about Hank."

Dave met me halfway down the hall, and I suddenly felt woozy. I grabbed his arm to keep from falling over, and he braced himself against the wall.

"Whoa, I'm dizzy," he said.

My mind raced. What was that smell?

It was like rotten eggs . . . or sulfur.

Oh no. I'd encountered this before. "Hold your breath!" I yelled. "Who else is in here?"

Dave's eyes widened. "Kim's setting up for a class, and Petunia's in the office."

"Gas leak," I said, "we need to get them out."

We raced down the hall. My lungs burned for lack of air, but I knew I couldn't take another breath. If I did, I might pass out.

And if we passed out here, with no one to help us, we'd die. My babies would die. And Laurie would be without a mother.

Kim bolted out of a classroom, her eyes wide. "What's that smell—"

I beckoned wildly toward the front. "Get out!" I hissed. "Don't breathe!"

She blinked twice, and then sprinted for the exit.

I ran faster. Dave and I burst into the office. Petunia had made it halfway to the door before she collapsed. I knelt next to her, but Dave picked her up effortlessly and ran back toward the hall. I followed, my lungs feeling like they were about to explode. Blackness beaded around the edges of my vision, and I felt so, so dizzy. I collided into the wall, then righted myself and made one final lunge for the outside.

Gasping for breath, I shoved my way through the door. Sweet, life-giving air poured into my lungs, and I shouted at a passerby, "Call 911!"

"Petunia!" Dave cried, his voice ragged. "Petunia, wake up!"

Nearby, Kim was on her hands and knees, retching.

I crawled over to Dave and Petunia. "Is she breathing?" I asked. Grabbing her arms, I felt for a pulse. There. She definitely had a pulse, and her chest was rising and falling, albeit shallowly.

"We need an ambulance and the fire department!" Dave yelled. His voice dropped to a mutter. "Wake up, wake up, wake up."

Still no response.

"Oh my God, no." Dave was desperate now. "Petunia! Stay with me, you hear? We're going to get married and have three kids, and they're all going to be beautiful like you and pro dancers and take over the studio when we retire. Stay with me. Please, baby. Don't go."

Petunia stirred and started coughing. I squeezed Dave's shoulder. "She's going to be fine," I whispered.

Her eyes fluttered open, and she whispered, "We're going to get married?"

"Yes, baby," Dave said, almost gasping out the words. "Absolutely." He bent toward her, and their lips met. Her hand reached up weakly to caress his cheek, and they shared a long, passionate kiss. I looked away to give them privacy.

In the distance, sirens wailed, and I waved down the fire trucks as they pulled into the parking lot. "Gas leak!" I yelled. "In that unit. Everyone's out."

An ambulance pulled in behind them, and paramedics attended Petunia as the firefighters evacuated the nearby units.

A pair of firefighters herded us to the far side of the parking lot, and I lay back on the pavement and rested my hand on my baby bump.

That had been close. Way too close.

A few minutes later, a tall African-American firefighter with broad shoulders and a calm demeanor found Dave and me. "You own the studio that had the leak?" he asked.

Dave nodded. "That's me."

The firefighter whistled. "You guys called it in just in time. Someone opened up the main line. A couple more minutes, and the whole building might have blown up."

CHAPTER 19

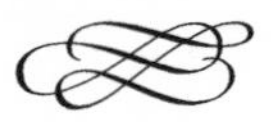

Jim pulled me into a tight hug the moment he walked into our house. "I'm so glad you're safe."

"I almost took Laurie there today," I whispered. "She would have been with me if Paula hadn't volunteered her mom to watch her."

"Where's Laurie now?" Jim asked urgently.

"Paula's mom is bringing her by in a couple hours. But . . . can you imagine?"

Jim swallowed. "We need a nanny and a backup nanny. We can't leave you in the position of hauling Laurie around on the job. There's too much danger in your line of work."

It was a reiteration of the decision we'd already made, but it felt more real this time. Personal. Irrevocable.

Someone banged on the door, and Jim held up a hand to signal me to stay on the couch. He peeked through a window at the front porch, and then let out a sigh of relief. "It's just Kenny."

"Speaking of nannies and backup nannies," I murmured.

Jim opened the door, and Kenny practically flew into the room, his eyes wide and his hands trembling. "I heard about the gas line leak on the news on the way home from filming with Odette. Were you there?" he asked.

"Yeah, but everyone's fine," I said. "Petunia was knocked out, but just briefly. She woke up before the paramedics even got there."

Kenny bit down hard on his lip. "Good. I'm so glad. Man." He ran a hand through his pink hair. "This whole case has really been something, huh?"

"You can say that again." I let out a long sigh.

"Is the fundraiser still on?" Jim asked, sitting back down beside me.

"Yes, it's still on," I said, staring at the wall. "They've closed the studio for the day to air it out, but they say it'll be safe by tomorrow morning."

"But will it really be safe if the killer is still on the loose?" Jim asked.

I sighed. "At least it gives me a new angle to look into. We can figure out who has an alibi for this morning and who doesn't."

Kenny shifted from foot to foot, looking more uncomfortable than I'd ever seen him.

"What is it?" I asked, studying him.

He opened his mouth and then closed it again, as if conflicted. Then he blurted, "I lied after Leo was murdered. Odette wasn't with me the whole time. She left to get us coffee, but the line was really long so she was gone for an hour. As soon as we found the body, she panicked and asked me to be her alibi and I said yes." He closed his eyes. "That's why I've been avoiding you and spending all my time with her. I felt guilty. I knew I shouldn't have done it. But I just knew she was innocent and didn't want her put through the ringer."

I blinked, trying to process what Kenny was saying. "So, Odette has no alibi for a significant portion of the window in which Leo was killed?"

"And there's more," he said through gritted teeth. "She went to get coffee right around the time Paula was hit over the head. And today, too, right before the gas leak. Both times, we were filming close to the studio, in front of a cool graffiti wall she told me about. After I heard about the gas leak, I . . . called her to ask for an explanation, and she just started screaming at me, saying I didn't trust her and that we were through."

My mind spun on this new information. What if . . .

A thunderous pounding sound from the garage practically shook the house. I massaged my temples. Could Jo-Jo not leave me a minute to think? Not one single, solitary minute?

"Kate?" Kenny interjected.

"Yeah?"

"I'm really, really, really sorry. I know it was an awful thing for me to do." His shoulders slumped.

"Oh, Kenny. I forgive you. Just don't do it again. And *especially* don't lie to the police again. You can get in a lot of trouble for that, you know."

"I know," he said, and I was reminded of how young he truly was.

I excused myself to the backyard and called Galigani.

"Yeah?" came his gruff voice over the line.

I sank into a chair beneath the pergola, the string lights casting an incandescent glow over everything. "You won't believe what Kenny just told me."

After I explained the story, Galigani said, "Hmm. That's troubling. So, she had opportunity, and her first impulse when she saw Leo was to beg for an alibi."

"People do crazy things when they're under stress, but that seemed weird to me too." I drummed my fingernails on the table.

"Plus, she's gone missing both times the saboteur has struck since the murder."

"If she isn't involved, that's a pretty darn big coincidence."

Galigani whistled. "You bet it is. I'll call McNearny and have Odette brought in for questioning. You'll need to send Kenny down to the precinct to tell them everything he knows, too."

"You don't think they'd charge him for lying to an officer, do you?" I asked, my breath catching.

"Nah," said Galigani, clearing his throat. "Not with McNearny handling the case. He just wants to catch the murderer. If the killer turns out to be Odette, he'll take into account Kenny's age and the way she manipulated him, and there'll be leniency. If she'd succeeded in killing anyone else in the meantime, it might have been a different story, of course. McNearny will probably want to scare Kenny onto the straight and narrow, though."

"Fine by me," I muttered.

We hung up, and when I went back inside, Kenny and Jim were standing near the front door.

"You really need to go give your statement to police tonight," I said. "Go voluntarily. Don't wait until they bring you in. It will look a lot better for you."

Kenny gulped but nodded. "Okay."

"The whole truth," I warned him. "Don't leave anything out. Give them your full cooperation."

"I will," he promised. "And I'm going to watch Laurie tomorrow for you free of charge! You don't even have to order me a pizza!"

I laughed. "Paying for pizza is the least of my worries!" I said, as he headed out. I peeked through the window to watch him leave, and sighed in relief when he went straight to his car instead of to his house. "Good," I murmured. "He's going to the precinct right away."

"So?" Jim asked with a grim look on his face.

I shrugged. "She had ample opportunity, and she's been acting suspiciously. That's all we know for sure. But, in any case, I bet they're broken up for good this time, and that's a mercy."

* * *

I SLEPT RESTLESSLY AND GROANED WHEN I WOKE UP TO A TEXT FROM Galigani saying police hadn't been able to locate Odette. Dread curdled in my stomach.

There was probably a reasonable explanation. She'd gone out after breaking up with Kenny and met someone to have a fling with, and they'd spent the night at his apartment rather than hers.

Or she'd gone to a girlfriend's place to eat ice cream and talk about her feelings.

Or she knew that police were onto her, and she was scheming her last and final revenge.

Kenny arrived to watch Laurie, looking appropriately subdued. "That one cop—you know, the one Deb calls Sergeant McGrumpy?"

I snorted. "Yeah, McNearny's his real name."

"Yeah, that one. He read me the riot act. But I'm just relieved to have gotten it all off my chest. It ate at me all the time. Especially at night. I've really had a hard time sleeping recently."

I almost retorted that I'd had a hard time sleeping, too, because I'd been hitting dead end after dead end in the case, but I erred on the side of grace. Kenny clearly felt terrible, and there was no reason to make him feel worse. What was done was done—and next time he'd think twice about covering for someone just because she had a pretty face.

Hopefully the whole experience made him wiser.

* * *

I HUMMED THE THEME TO *SWAN LAKE* AS JIM AND I DROVE TO *TRE Fratelli Danzanti*. The studio was a frenzy of activity—this was an all-hands-on-board event. Paula, dressed to the nines and showing no sign of her concussion, was directing a handful of dance teachers who were setting up tables. Kim was among them, her dark hair pulled back in a ponytail and a look of determination on her face.

Dave practically bounced up to us. "No such thing as bad publicity," he crowed. "We've sold every last ticket. The place will be packed. And I upsold about thirty percent of the attendees to a package of ballroom dance classes. We've never had so many students on the books."

"I'm so glad," said Jim.

"We'll be able to pay for Sharon's treatment and set the studio up for a great fiscal year." Dave's face grew more serious. "And police have agreed to be undercover in the crowd, watching for anything suspicious, so the event should be safe."

"Fingers crossed," I said weakly.

Petunia pushed a janitor's cart out of the bathroom, sweat beading on her brow. She waved at us and called, "We've got this!"

How I hoped she was right. I was pretty sure we'd cracked the case —but I just hoped I wasn't too late.

"Darling!" Mom called from the direction of the lobby. "Could you help me bring some of this food inside?"

I dispatched Jim to assist Mom for me and went to ask Paula what

I could do to help. Anything to get my mind off the fact that police couldn't find Odette.

"Could you set that out front?" Paula called, waving me toward an A-frame sign in the same style as the posters Jim had designed—the silhouetted swing dance couple, the calligraphy-style font, and . . .

"No!" I gasped aloud.

In huge letters at the top, there it was again: *PUBIC DANCE.*

"Paula!" I shrieked.

She glanced at me with a quizzical expression, and I gestured wildly at the sign.

"Read it!" I yelled.

"Public dance," she said aloud.

"Spell it," I insisted.

She furrowed her brow, "P-u-b-i . . . oh my stars." Her eyes popped wide open. "We can't get that reprinted in time! I . . . I don't know how that happened! I pulled it from the file Jim sent, so it would match the posters."

I groaned aloud. "From the draft poster? Did he send it to you to look it over?"

"Yeah. I said it looked great."

"Okay," I said, folding my hands together. "We can fix this. We don't need a fancy A-frame sign. What should we use instead, that we can put together at the last minute?"

Paula stared at me with a look of panic on her face. "Um. Um. I'm sorry. I've had crazy brain fog since I got knocked out. I—"

"Take a deep breath." I pulled her into a hug. "I'll take care of this. Just focus on getting the interior laid out the way you want."

"Okay," she said, inhaling sharply. "Thank you. I trust you implicitly."

I leaned against the wall and ran a Google search on my phone for cute 1950s sign ideas. And then it hit me. "A chalkboard!" I cried. "Like what you might see at a soda fountain."

Paula whirled toward me. "That's perfect!"

"Do we have anyone who can do the lettering?" I asked.

"I can do that," Hank said from behind me.

I turned, and Hank had his arm around the shoulders of one of the dance teachers.

"Kate," he said, "this is my niece, Dara. She's a new instructor here."

Ah, this must be the niece who'd been teaching at Dare to Dance until recently. I extended my hand. "It's so nice to meet you, Dara."

Hank continued, "I've got a pretty good knack for lettering, and I think I can make the chalkboard look like it came straight out of the fifties. How about I go track a board down and take care of setting it up?"

"Thank you!" Paula called. "I have the best friends!"

The day passed in a whirlwind, but I kept checking my phone to see if there were any updates on Odette. Finally, midway through the afternoon, I called Deb.

"Yo, Kate," Deb said when she answered.

"Hey, Deb," I said. "Are you on the job tonight at the swing dance?"

"You bet," she said. "I'm going undercover as a partygoer. McGrumpy's coming, too. He's posing as my date." Distaste colored her voice.

Then we both howled in laughter.

"Well, maybe if we can find the killer, you can ditch McNearny and find a lovely lady to dance with."

"I sure hope so," she said dreamily.

"Speaking of the case, any progress on tracking down Odette?" I crossed my fingers and hoped against hope for a break.

"Zip, zilch, nada. It's like the girl vanished into thin air."

I didn't like this. Not one bit.

"But get this. We talked to some of her friends and found out that she's been dating this anesthesiologist, and his office had a whole bottle of vecuronium bromide go missing two weeks ago."

My mind stuttered on *she's been dating this anesthesiologist*. "Did the friends say anything about her dating a younger musician?"

"Not a word," said Deb flatly. "And that's not all. We talked to the baristas at the coffee shop, and we took a look at their online records and video feed. The day of the killing, our Ms. Malakhova put in a pickup order via their app for four coffees. She was in and out of the coffee shop in thirty seconds, but she told your kid babysitter that the line had taken her an hour to get through."

I'd been right. Odette had definitely just been using Kenny. I pursed my lips. I was really starting to hate her. I took a deep breath. "A missing bottle of vecuronium bromide. What are the odds?"

"Pretty darn slim, if you ask me. We're watching for anything suspicious tonight, of course, but we will most definitely be looking out for Odette in particular. If anyone sees her, they need to flag us down ASAP."

"Noted. I'll pass the word around." Then my brain latched onto the name Deb had called Odette. "Did you say *Ms. Malakhova*?"

"Yeah. Odette Malakhova."

"Is that her birth name?" I demanded.

Deb paused, and I heard a few keyboard keys clack in the background. "Yeah, it's her birth name."

"Is her middle name Giselle, by any chance?"

"No, it's Anya." Then she let out a whoop. "But she has a sister named Giselle. Or, had one. The sister's deceased. Why?"

Giselle Malakhova. The girl Todd had been suspected of poisoning.

"A hunch," I said.

Deb chuckled. "All right. Keep your secrets, and we'll track her down and bring her in. See you tonight!"

I made sure that everyone knew to be on the lookout for Odette, and mused over the case while absentmindedly following Paula's instructions.

Years earlier, Todd had been a suspect in the poisoning of Odette's now-deceased sister. And now he and Odette were working together at the same studio? These pieces fit together somehow. I was certain of it. But how?

What if Leo had just been collateral damage? What if Odette was trying to kill Todd?

After another hour or so of preparation, the studio looked perfect. The dividers had been rolled back, revealing a huge dance floor, decorated to a tee, with tables and chairs around the edges. Paula and I high-fived.

"You did good," I told her, swelling with pride at my best friend's talent.

"It was a team effort!" she said, throwing her arms around me.

Jim and I headed home to get ready for the dance, and on the way out, I inspected Hank's hand-chalked sign. It looked exactly like an old soda fountain chalkboard. His lettering was excellent—and most importantly, he'd spelled *PUBLIC* correctly.

I let out a sigh of relief. That was one problem taken care of.

Now we just had to keep our eyes open for Odette—perhaps she should have been named Odile, after *Swan Lake's* villainous Black Swan.

We pulled into the driveway at home, and I gasped out loud. Our front door was standing open, and Whiskers was crouched beneath a bush in the flower bed.

I glanced toward the street and then over at Kenny's house. Jo-Jo's truck was still here—the garage door was closed, though, which was odd—and Kenny's van was in his parents' driveway. Maybe Jo-Jo had left the front door open while going in or out, and Kenny had taken Laurie out to the backyard and hadn't noticed?

But a sick, panicky feeling in my stomach told me something was wrong.

Very, very wrong.

CHAPTER 20

Jim clambered out and hissed, "Stay in the car."

Not a chance. Not until I knew my baby was safe. I climbed out after Jim, snatched up Whiskers, and tossed her into our car. Then I darted into the house, almost colliding with Jim's back.

"Kenny?" Jim called. "Jo-Jo?"

Pure, sweet relief filled me when Laurie wailed. "Laurie!" I screamed, bolting toward her nursery. I hurtled through the door and found her lying in her crib, crying. I picked her up, searching her for any signs of injury. She was fine, but her diaper was absolutely soaked.

Murmuring nonsensical words to her in a soothing voice, I rejoined Jim in the living room.

"No one's here," he said, his face pale.

"Check the garage."

He strode to the door and opened it. "Oh no."

"What?" I asked, crowding behind him to see.

Jo-Jo was knocked out in the middle of the garage near a pile of two-by-fours. Next to him lay an empty medical syringe.

My blood pressure skyrocketed as I fumbled for my phone.

"Stay here," Jim ordered.

I nodded and dialed 911. "I need police and ambulance here right away," I said to the operator. "My babysitter is missing, and my contractor was attacked and knocked out. I'd bet anything he was poisoned with vercuronium bromide."

"Yes, ma'am, I'm dispatching someone to you right away," the operator responded in a voice that seemed entirely too calm for the situation. "Hold tight. You said your babysitter is missing? Is there a child in the home?"

"Yes, my daughter's fine. I have her. She was in her crib."

"Kate!" Jim called.

I hung up on 911 and ran to meet Jim at the back door. He was staring into the yard with a horrified look on his face. I followed his gaze.

Beneath the pergola, Odette stood holding a knife to Kenny's throat. My heart lurched at the wide-eyed look of terror on his face. I covered Laurie's eyes.

"Stay back!" Odette shrieked, a maniacal light gleaming in her eyes. "Don't get any closer! I'll kill him."

I tightened my grip on Laurie and took a step away from the knife-wielding fiend. "It's going to be okay, Kenny."

Jim called, "Give it up, Odette. Police are already on their way."

Odette's eyes darted to Jim, and I took the chance to slip my phone out of my pocket. Holding it behind Laurie so Odette couldn't see, I dialed Galigani, put my phone on speaker and then hit the mute button.

Please let this work!

Swallowing my fear, I choked out, "Why'd you kill Leo, Odette?"

Odette's grip on Kenny tightened. "No one would have ever found out if this snitch hadn't opened his big mouth."

"Listen," I said, trying to keep my voice as soothing as possible, "I can help you. I have friends on the force and I know the best defense attorney in town. I'm sure he can get you a good plea deal. Help me help you. Tell me what happened."

She hissed, "It was never supposed to be Leo. The fool ruined my whole plan when he stole the coffee. But, you know, play stupid games, win stupid prizes, I guess."

Todd. I was right. She'd been going after Todd. "Who was supposed to die?" I asked, affecting confusion.

Odette barked a harsh laugh. "You want to help me get a plea deal? I can get my own deal. Because I just have to tell them the truth. They'll feel bad for me. They'll give me a deal. Leo was never supposed to die. I was going to get sweet, sweet revenge for what he did to Giselle."

"Giselle?" I asked softly.

"My older sister," said Odette sourly. "Unlike me, she followed our parents' dreams for her life and danced ballet, until Todd's poison left her too sick and traumatized to keep going. She killed herself two years ago."

My stomach dropped.

Suicide. My heart broke for their poor family. "I'm so sorry about Giselle," I said, and even though Odette was absolutely crazed, I meant every word. "That's terrible."

The words poured out of her faster now. "So, I tracked Todd down. I uprooted my life in New York and moved to San Francisco to take a job at this studio so that I could watch him and wait for the right moment. I was patient. I watched every move he made. When he started talking to Monte, I knew. So, I started talking to Monte, too. That idiot was even going to give me a tidy payday if I brought down *Tre Fratelli Danzanti.* So, I figured, why not do two things at once? No one would look twice at me after they learned Todd was scheming against the studio and Kim was reluctant to go along with it." Her face contorted in rage. "And then that loser Leo went and stole the coffee. He ruined everything."

Man, oh man, I hoped Galigani—or his voicemail—was getting all this.

"Did Monte know about the murder?" I asked gently, trying to calm her, worried she'd hurt Kenny in her agitation.

"No," she scoffed. "He didn't have the stomach for that sort of thing. I told him that Leo died of a heart attack and I'd made it look like a murder to make the studio look bad, lose its students, be forced to close down. He was so uncomfortable. I've never seen anyone squirm like that. But he kept his mouth shut because he knew no one would believe that he wasn't involved."

"Were you the one who hit Paula over the head?" Jim demanded.

Odette smirked.

"You shouldn't have done that," Kenny said in a strained voice. "Kate's mom told me Paula was wearing Kate's jacket. And you'd made an excuse to go get coffee then too. What were the odds? And then again, right before the studio almost blew up. Why were you always getting coffee when bad things happened?"

"Shut up," growled Odette. "I just wanted to slow Kate down. She wasn't even the target of the gas leak."

I furrowed my brow. "Who was?"

Odette just smirked.

Then it hit me. "Kim," I said, my voice raspy. "You were targeting Kim." The realization unfolded like a flower in bloom. "The coffee was never for Todd. You didn't want to kill him. At least not yet. You wanted him to suffer the way you'd suffered, losing someone he loved."

That cold smile never left her face.

Kenny locked eyes with me, and a look of pure determination crossed his face. He dropped his center of gravity low, getting his neck clear of the knife, and then stomped on Odette's foot.

Odette shrieked and lunged toward him. He fell backward, out of reach of the swooping knife, and scrambled away.

A siren wailed nearby. Odette pulled up short, panic overtaking her features. Then she ran toward Jim, Laurie, and me.

Jim lurched protectively toward us, pushing us out of the way. But Odette wasn't aiming for us. She flew through the door into the house.

"She's getting away!" yelled Kenny.

"Stay here," Jim growled as he raced after her.

Kenny tailed Jim and I trailed with Laurie at a safer distance.

The front door banged open and closed. When I reached the driveway, cautiously behind Jim and Kenny, I saw the strangest sight. In the soft glow of dusk, red-and-white lights cast an eerie almost-flicker over the scene. Odette lay on the ground, unconscious. And Jo-Jo was holding a two-by-four and rubbing his head while he glared down at her.

"Crazy lassie," he muttered.

First four cop cars and then an ambulance pulled into the driveway.

"Jo-Jo!" I yelled. "Are you all right? Are you poisoned?"

"Nah," he said, his Irish lilt even thicker than usual. "She tried, but I knocked the needle out of her hand. Then she got ahold of a hammer and hit me over the head. Crazy, crazy lass."

"Hands in the air!" yelled a cop, hand on his gun.

We all raised our hands, and I called, "It's fine. The woman who's knocked out is the culprit. She's also guilty of the murder at that dance studio in the Mission District. Call Detective Deb Fisher. She'll vouch for our story."

The cops confirmed our stories and then took our statements. Jo-Jo waved off the paramedics, saying he just needed to go home and sleep it off.

"I'll feel grand by tomorrow," he insisted.

An hour later, the police hauled a now-awake Odette away in handcuffs. The Black Swan shot a venomous glare at all of us, but saved the worst of her poison for Kenny.

"You worthless idiot," she screamed. "You don't know a thing about loyalty!"

They closed her into the squad car and drove off.

Kenny sighed and brushed his hands on his jeans.

"You okay?" I asked.

"Dodged a bullet there, didn't I?"

"It can still hurt."

He tilted his head and thought for a moment. "It doesn't. Nothing to give you closure like being held at knifepoint." He glanced at his phone. "Oh! The dance! You're running late!"

The dance! In the commotion, I'd entirely forgotten. And I was supposed to help teach some of the beginners. I'd already missed that.

But it was better to skip the dance—I couldn't make Kenny babysit after what he'd just been through, and Dave and Petunia and Jack and Eddie would understand under the circumstances. So, I just waved my hand and said, "Oh, we don't have to worry about that. Why don't you go get some rest, and we'll have a quiet evening with Laurie?"

Kenny shook his head vehemently. "No way. You worked so hard on that dance, and now you've saved it from a crazy killer. You deserve to see everything that you've worked for." He reached out for Laurie, and she happily went to him. "Miss Laurie and I will have a great evening."

"You sure?" Jim asked.

"Go get ready!" Kenny said, laughing. "I'll take Laurie over to my mom's. We all watch a movie and eat kettle-style popcorn. That's vegan and approved."

"Not Laurie," I gasped. "She could choke."

Kenny shook his head. "Not Laurie, nah. She can have a mashed banana. That's vegan too." He plucked a sleepy Laurie out of my arms. "Plus, Ma's been texting me. She saw the cops out front. So, we'll all hang out together tonight. Safety in numbers."

Jim clapped Kenny on the back. "Thanks, Kenny, for keeping Laurie safe. You're a good man."

At the mention of the word *man*, Kenny's chest magically puffed up like a rooster and I hid a smile.

Jim rushed off to get dressed, and I saw Kenny and Laurie to the door.

"We won't be too late, Kenny. Thank you."

After closing my front door, I raced to get dressed, reprising my film noir Samantha Spade, Private Eye look. After another case in the books, I'd earned it. As soon as I put on my lipstick, I looked in the mirror and said in my best Humphrey Bogart voice, "I don't mind a reasonable amount of trouble."

"What's that?" Jim called from the other room.

"Nothing!" I replied, reaching for my curling iron.

As I finished curling my hair, Jim came up behind me and put his hands on my waist. "You look sexy," he purred.

"So do you," I said. "But sexy isn't going to save you from a curling iron burn if you get your face any closer to my hair."

"Fair enough. You about ready?"

"Just two more curls." I held up two fingers.

"I'll start the car."

CHAPTER 21

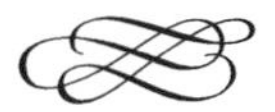

We pulled up to the dance at the same time as Galigani.

"You did good, kid," Galigani said when we got out of the car.

"You got my call?" I asked hopefully.

"Every word. Recorded it, too, and sent it off to McNearny before I came here. That will be enough to put her away, especially after they test the coffee stains on Leo's shirt for vercuronium bromide."

I threw my arms around him. "Couldn't have done it without you."

He stiffened at first, then patted my shoulder. When I pulled away, a soft, fatherly smile lit up his face. "You're made for this work, you know."

"Really?" Such a compliment from the usually understated Galigani warmed me all the way to my core.

He grunted, and then added, "Don't let it go to your head. Let's go inside. I've had some time to think about what's really important to me, and I've got a surprise up my sleeve."

"A surprise? How mysterious," I said.

Jim laughed and slung an arm around my shoulder, and the three of us walked past Hank's hand-chalked sign and into the studio. The lobby was made up to look like a diner, with a chalked menu board that matched the sign out front. That must have been another last-minute idea from Hank.

"Welcome to the dance," said Kim from behind the front desk. She gestured to the chalkboard with a wink. "Can I interest you in any of our house specials? Twenty percent off before the clock strikes midnight!"

"Yeah," said Galigani, "I'll take you up on that."

Looking more closely at the menu, I realized it was a list of *Tre Fratelli Danzanti's* dance classes.

"What a great idea!" I breathed. Then I stared at Galigani like he had two heads. "You're signing up for *dance classes?*"

He shrugged. "Your mom likes to dance. I'm not any good at it and didn't want to embarrass myself, but that's why you take lessons, isn't it?"

He pointed to an item on the menu and pulled out his credit card. "Let's do Intro to Ballroom for Couples."

"Group, semi-private, or private?" Kim asked.

Galigani's brow creased, and he looked pained. "Better go private," he grumbled. "I don't need to embarrass myself in front of *everybody*."

While Kim rang him up, I asked her, "So, how are sales going? Dave said you guys were pretty booked out even before tonight."

She practically glowed as she replied, "We're going to hire a half a dozen new teachers to keep up with demand. And"—her smile grew almost devious—"I talked to an investigative journalist today about Todd and Monte's underhanded scheming. He thought it was a great story to run alongside coverage of the murder. By the time the press is through with Dare to Dance, I think we'll be buying *them* out."

I high-fived her, and then Galigani, Jim, and I headed into the hall, toward the crooning of jazz music. The dance hall was packed with couples, some expertly lindy-hopping like trained pros and other struggling to execute a basic rock step. But the energy was electric, and everyone looked like they were having a blast.

Nearby, Paula and her husband David were dancing a respectable triple-step, and I ran to them and tapped David on the shoulder.

"Mind if I cut in?" I asked, grinning. I grabbed Paula's hands and spun her in a circle. "It looks perfect!"

We collapsed into a fit of giggles, and she called over the music, "Did you really catch Odette? It's all over?"

"It's all over."

Her shoulders slumped in relief. "Thank goodness." Then she perked up. "Oh, did you see the food table?" She herded me to the edge of the room, and on the way, I spotted Deb dancing with a pretty thirtysomething brunette. I waved at them as we passed, and Deb grinned at me. "Yo! Great job on the case! It's nice to be off duty!"

I knew Deb well enough to recognize the signs that she was already halfway to inebriated, and I suspected she was making considerable use of the cash bar. I made a mental note to call her a cab at the end of the night.

At about the midpoint of the dance hall, three long tables were heaped with food.

"My gosh," I said to Paula. "Mom didn't do all of this, did she?"

Paula said in my ear, "When he heard how many tickets we'd sold, Hank paid for a caterer to supplement the food, so we could have enough for everyone without cutting into the studio's profits. *And* he paid them extra to put all the stuff your mom made front and center to showcase her talents."

Sure enough, in the center of the middle table, three small white pillars supported platters of the food Mom had made—funky, fun molded Jell-O desserts, salmon dip, and a pineapple upside-down cake with a maraschino cherry tucked inside each pineapple ring.

In front of the pillar was a little plaque with a photo and bio of Mom.

That *was* really sweet of Hank.

I thought of Vicente's gambling allegations and pursed my lips. I was going to have to check into that.

But even if it turned out Vicente was one hundred percent wrong and Hank hadn't threatened anyone at poker night, I was always and forever Team Galigani.

Cheers rang out behind us, and we turned to see a circle open up around Dave and Petunia, who were improvising a lindy-hop routine that would have been right at home at the international championships. Petunia, of course, wore a floral dress, and two dozen flowers were pinned in her thick, curly black hair. But what I noticed most was how radiant she looked. Their dancing took my breath away.

Out of the corner of my eye, I caught sight of Mom and Hank dancing. I searched the crowd for Galigani but didn't see him.

Jim joined Paula and me, and the three of us watched Dave and Petunia finish out the song. They struck the final pose, and we cheered along with the watching crowd. Then a quieter, slower song started, and Dave pulled a ring box out of his pocket, grabbed Petunia's hand, and dropped to one knee.

I didn't have a hope of hearing the proposal over the whoops of the enthusiastic onlookers, but tears brimmed in Petunia's eyes as she screamed, "*Yes!*"

Dave slid the ring on her finger, then jumped to his feet and dipped her. Their lips met in a passionate kiss, and when he righted her, he held up his hand and yelled, "We're getting married!"

That's when I saw Galigani on the far side of Mom and Hank. My breath caught in my throat. What was Galigani holding? It looked like . . . a ring box of his own.

Galigani looked at Dave and Petunia, then at Mom and Hank, and slipped the ring box back into his pocket. He caught me staring and shook his head. "Not now," he mouthed. "Later."

I jerked my head toward Mom and Hank and trained an intense look on Galigani. He swallowed, his Adam's apple visibly bobbing even from this distance. Then he approached Mom and Hank. He tapped Hank on the shoulder, and Mom's smile was radiant as he reached out and took her hand.

Hank looked disappointed, but a moment later, his niece dragged him into the throng of dancers.

Dave and Petunia ran up to us, and Petunia was practically glowing. Dave pulled Jim into a hug. "You'll be my best man?"

"Of course," Jim said. "I'm so happy for you guys. You deserve this."

Then Dave looked at me and said, "Detective Fisher said you solved the case!"

"Just in the nick of time," I replied.

"Look over there." He pointed into the crowd, and I spotted Jack and Sharon dancing. Sharon was every bit as radiant as Petunia.

Petunia squealed, "We made enough to pay for the fertility treatments and then some. They have a real shot at having a baby!"

"And"—Dave looked at me and fist-pumped the air—"there's a whole lot left over. The deal was half of the fundraiser proceeds, after whatever we raised for Jack and Sharon. Between the ticket sales and the proceeds from the cash bar, we're going to owe you a pretty big paycheck."

"Oh!" I exclaimed. I'd forgotten about the financial agreement—I hadn't expected there to be much, if any, money left over, but all the publicity had made the event a smashing success.

Eddie pulled Dave and Petunia away to congratulate them, and Jim looked at me and exclaimed, "Hey, that's really going to help us with hiring the nanny."

"I'm getting paychecks from clients just like you told me to!" I declared triumphantly.

Another slow song played, and Jim pointed up to the ceiling and said, "I think even my rhythmless self can handle this one." He held out his hand. "May I have this dance?"

"You may," I said with a soft smile.

Jim took my hand and pulled me close, my baby bump cradled between us. We swayed to the music, and the world seemed perfect. When the last notes of the song faded away, he pulled me into dip and kissed me until my head spun.

To Do:

1. Interview nannies.
2. Check into Hank's gambling.
3. Find Wonder Woman thing for Nick's wife? What do nerds like?
4. Help Galigani figure out how to propose to Mom.
5. Offer Jo-Jo hazard pay.
6. Land another paying client.

READY FOR MORE?

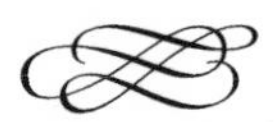

Book 9 from Maternal Instincts…

Click here to get your copy now.

PREVIEW OF PRAMS & POISON

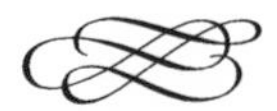

CHAPTER 1

o Do:

1. Take Laurie to puppet time at the library.
2. Furnish twins' new nursery!
3. Interview prospective nannies.
4. Dinner Saturday with Nick and his wife.
5. Buy larger maternity clothes!
6. Land new paying client.
7. Find out if Hank's poker night is on the up and up.

"PAULA!" I HELD OUT MY ARMS TO WELCOME MY BEST FRIEND TO MY recently beautified backyard. My wonderful husband Jim had worked with Jojo—the contractor doing our garage-turned-nursery renovation—to turn the raggedy, neglected space into an oasis.

Even in the middle of the day, when the string lights draped between the house and the pergola didn't cast their fairytale glow on everything, I loved it.

Paula's jaw dropped as she pushed the pram through the gate and over the rippling grass. "You weren't kidding! Jim did such a great job on this."

Baby Chloe's tiny face peeked out of the pram from amid a sea of polka-dotted blankets, and Paula's two-year-old Danny trailed behind them, zooming his toy through the air while making a high-pitched whirring noise.

Laurie flailed in my arms at the sight of her little friends and managed to land a painful kick on my growing baby bump.

"Hey!" I said, resting my free hand on my abdomen. "Be nice to your little siblings, peanut."

She just wiggled some more.

Paula pulled the pram to a halt beneath the pergola, and Danny leaped from the stroller, holding his Spider Man action figure high in the air.

"I'm Pie-da Man!" he yelled, throwing out his hand like he was shooting a web at me.

"Whoa!" I staggered back as if he'd hit me, then sank to my knees in the grass.

With a grin, Paula pointed him toward a little patch of dirt in the corner—the garden Jim and I had always intended to cultivate but hadn't gotten around to. "Can you play nicely for Auntie Kate for a second while I go get Paws?"

He stopped and stared up at his mom. Then he yelled, "Pie-da Man," and bolted for the garden.

Paula shook her head and pulled down her huge sunglasses to glance at me. "I cannot believe what I was thinking, adding a puppy to this chaos. But oh my word, Kate, I have *so* much to tell you!"

"I want to hear about that mysterious client you hinted about in your text," I called as she retreated toward the gate.

"Back in one minute!" she yelled.

I set Laurie in the corner of the garden, warning Danny sternly to be gentle and not throw the action figure at her. He ignored me and banged the Spider Man headfirst into the sand.

"Good enough," I muttered, walking backward toward Chloe's stroller while keeping a wary eye on Danny and Laurie. I loved

Danny, but he was a rough-and-tumble three-year-old, and I was always a little worried he was going to knock her over or bite her.

Just as I reached the stroller and unbuckled Chloe, Paula returned to the yard, her chocolate lab puppy straining at the leash.

"Paws!" Paula snapped in the warning voice that meant she was down to her last nerve. "Sit!"

Paws did not sit.

Groaning, Paula pulled the gate closed behind her. "Mind if I take him off his leash so he can get some of his energy out?"

"Be my guest," I said, bouncing Chloe and heading back toward the kiddos, who were happily playing in the dirt. The yard wasn't huge by any means—space was at a premium in San Francisco—but Paws's desperate desire to run was almost palpable.

Paula unhooked the leash from his collar. The little dog let out a jubilant yelp and tore around the perimeter of the yard, his tail thrashing back and forth in unbridled glee.

"He's pretty cute," I said. I hadn't met Paws before—he was a brand-new addition to Paula's family.

"He's trouble," she said in a wry voice, reaching for Chloe. "I'm pretty sure he's going to end up chewing the leg off the couch. And look at this!" She held out her forearms and showed me a set of four healing scratches. "These are from his nails! Did you know puppy claws are that sharp?"

I handed the baby over and sat down in the dirt next to Danny and Laurie, not caring that I was getting my joggers and oversize sweatshirt messy. Paula, who was wearing dark-wash skinny jeans and an impossibly fashionable slouchy blazer, stayed standing, several feet back from the garden.

"So," I said, tracing a line in the dirt in front of Laurie, "your new client?"

With a squeal, Paula said, "You will not *believe* this! I landed a gig as the designer for a renovation of one of the Painted Ladies!"

"Shut. Up!" I yelled, a huge grin on my face. "That's amazing!"

Paula had been working hard to build her interior design business, and the Painted Ladies—a set of Victorian- and Edwardian-style homes refinished in vivid colors and featured on literally zillions of postcards—were absolutely iconic.

"It's a one-in-a-lifetime opportunity," she raved. "A chance to leave my mark on a unique piece of classic San Francisco. I just hope I can do it justice. I'm meeting with the clients tomorrow to look at the house."

"You deserve every bit of this success," I said firmly.

Paws zipped across the dirt patch, kicking a cloud of dust up into my face. A ticklish sensation in my nose overpowered me, and I sneezed. The four-legged troublemaker turned around and jumped up on me, his paws connecting with my shoulders and knocking me off balance.

"Paws!" scolded Paula.

But I just laughed and sat back up, brushing myself off. "Maybe we should dampen the dirt a little so there's not so much dust. We've got a mister attachment on the hose that should do the job nicely."

Paula made a face but picked her way to the side of the house and gingerly picked up the hose.

"Twist it to the left," I called.

She turned on the hose and raced over to the garden, waving the hose in the general direction of the dirt patch. Too late, I realized the mister attachment was lying in the dirt at the side of the house. A stream of water burst from the end of the hose just as I pulled Laurie and Danny away.

Paws charged straight for the onslaught of water and tore head-first into the mud.

Paula shrieked and dropped the hose. "Oh no! Wet dog!" she wailed, running back to the side of the house and cranking off the hose. As the flow slowed, Paws settled at the end of the hose and licked up the last trickle of running water.

I covered my mouth. "I'm so sorry, Paula, the mister fell off." Glancing at Paws, I added, "At least he's already chocolate colored, so he doesn't look quite so muddy?"

"He just had a bath yesterday." She facepalmed dramatically.

I made a sympathetic noise in the back of my throat. "I'm sorry."

Out of the corner of my eye, movement lurched toward the muddy dirt patch. "Danny, stop—"

But it was too late. Danny had plopped himself on his back in the mud.

"Angel!" he yelled, throwing out his arms and legs like he was making a snow angel in a mud-wrestling pit.

Paula squeaked in horror.

Danny scrambled to his feet, giggling, and made a mad dash at Laurie and me. I shrieked and tried to dive out of the way, but he caught Laurie by the arm and tackled her to the ground, wrapping his muddy arms around her.

Laurie's eyes widened as if she wasn't sure whether to laugh or wail.

"You're all right, duck," I cooed in an upbeat voice. She stared at me. Then a smile stretched across her face, and she dissolved into a fit of riotous giggles.

One crisis averted.

Another . . . I took in the two extremely muddy children and even muddier puppy. Another crisis not-so-averted.

But mud washed off.

I met Paula's gaze, and a smirk tugged on the corners of her lips. "Another day in the life?" she offered in a high-pitched voice.

We burst into hysterical laughter. "The Mystery of the Muddy Mayhem," I managed to choke out.

Paula wiped tears from the corners of her eyes. "Oh boy. I needed a good laugh." Her nose wrinkled. "I'd have preferred it didn't come with a side of Gloppy the Mud Monster, but I'll take what I can get."

"Everything all right?" I asked, tilting my head to study her.

She waved her hand. "I'm stretched so thin. David is working all the time, and my mom's out of town, so I'm down a babysitter. I'm trying to build my business while taking care of two little ones—and for reasons I can't fathom, I added one extremely energetic and needy puppy to the mix. It'll pass. Just a season of being a little more tired."

"Well, you still look glamorous," I assured her. "Hey, my mom wanted some time with Laurie tomorrow. What if I rope her into babysitting your littles, too, and we can go look at your new project together?"

Relief flooded her face. "Oh, that'd be perfect. I've been scrambling to try to find someone—there's sure to be media around on a Painted Lady renovation, and I really want to look professional and put-together if a reporter wants to interview me. This is a huge career move."

Paula *always* looked professional and put-together. I opened my mouth to say just that, but before I could get the words out, Danny threw a stick at her.

The stick bounced harmlessly off her leg, and she turned to scold the toddler. "Hey. No throwing sticks. That can hurt people," she said firmly.

But my attention was fixed on Paws—because *his* attention was fixed on the stick. Paws charged the stick at Paula's feet.

She let out a screech and tried to back away, but at the last second, he abandoned the stick and reared up, catching her off balance. She tumbled backward into the grass with a little scream.

With a whimper of joy, Paws clambered up onto her and started licking her face, his feet tracking mud all over her perfectly fashionable blouse.

KEEP READING!

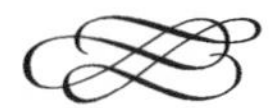

Book 9 from Maternal Instincts…

Click here to get your copy now.

OTHER TITLES BY DIANA ORGAIN

Maternal Instincts Mystery Series

Bundle of Trouble - FREE The only thing tougher than solving a murder… giving birth!

Motherhood is Murder Kate joins a new mom group where mischief and murder run rampant.

Formula for Murder A hit and run crash catapults Kate into a mystery at the French Consulate.

Nursing a Grudge Kate's budding PI business is threatened when a new PI poaches her client.

Pampered to Death Spa day has never been so deadly!

Killer Cravings Can Kate juggle being a PI, pregnant and those cravings all at the same time?

A Deathly Rattle Who shot rival PI, Vicente Domingo?

Rockabye Murder Dancing can be murder—literally.

Prams & Poison Are there too many skeletons in the Victorian closet Paula's is renovating?

Love or Money Mystery Series

A First Date with Death Reality TV meets murder!

A Second Chance at Murder Georgia's new boyfriend disappears in the Pyrenees Mountains.

Third Time's a Crime If only love were as simple as murder…

Roundup Crew Mystery Series

Yappy Hour Things take a *ruff* turn at the Wine & Bark when Maggie Patterson takes charge

Trigger Yappy Salmonella poisoning strikes at the Wine & Bark.

iWitch Mystery Series

A Witch Called Wanda Can a witch solve a murder mystery?

I Wanda put a spell on you When Wanda is kidnapped, Maeve might need a little magic.

Brewing up Murder A witch, a murder, a dog...no, wait...a man..no...two men, three witches and a cat?

Cooking Up Murder Mystery Series

Murder as Sticky as Jam Mona and Vicki are ready for the grand opening of Jammin' Honey until…their store goes up in smoke…

GET SELECT DIANA ORGAIN TITLES FOR FREE

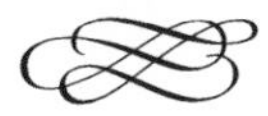

Building a relationship with my readers is one the things I enjoy best. I occasionally send out messages about new releases, special offers, discount codes and other bits of news relating to my various series.

And for a limited time, I'll send you copy of BUNDLE OF TROUBLE: Book 1 in the MATERNAL INSTINCTS MYSTERY SERIES.

Join now

ABOUT THE AUTHOR

Diana Orgain is the bestselling author of the *Maternal Instincts Mystery Series,* the *Love or Money Mystery Series,* and the *Roundup Crew Mysteries.* She is the co-author of NY Times Best-selling *Scrapbooking Mystery Series* with Laura Childs. For a complete listing of books, as well as excerpts and contests, and to connect with Diana:

Visit Diana's website at www.dianaorgain.com.

Join Diana reader club and newsletter and get Free books here